"Why can't they get a posse up? I mean, the man shot up three lawmen. They must want him pretty bad."

Weatherbee sighed. "Don't you get it, Raider? Beale knows me. He's going down there to tell Mantooth just who I am. I have to have some room to move around, too. If you're going to work undercover, you'll need to make contact."

A look came over Raider's face. He didn't say anything.

Before Doc knew it, he was gone...

Other books by
J. D. HARDIN

J.D. HARDIN

THE OZARK OUTLAWS

BERKLEY BOOKS, NEW YORK

THE OZARK OUTLAWS

A Berkley Book/published by arrangement with
the author

PRINTING HISTORY
Berkley edition/December 1984

ISBN: 0-425-07392-0

A BERKLEY BOOK ® TM 757,375
Berkley Books are published by Berkley Publishing Group,
200 Madison Avenue, New York, N.Y. 10016
The name "BERKLEY" and the stylized "B" with design are trademarks
belonging to Berkley Publishing Corporation.

PRINTED IN THE UNITED STATES OF AMERICA

CHAPTER ONE

The man's name was Peters. Jesse Peters. But no one would remember him beyond that dark day in late July. He was just another in a series of blunt-faced, round-shouldered ex-soldiers hired as guards by the Harrison Cartage Company. He had fought with the Confederate army at Elk Horn Tavern over at Pea Ridge, in Arkansas, and at Wilson's Creek, up in Missouri. After the war, he drifted, worked as a bartender in Joplin, a bouncer in Springfield, a day laborer in Harrison, Arkansas. Peters was thirty-two years old and had done nothing distinguished in his life.

Nor would he do much this day.

Peters was a man marked for death.

He didn't know this, of course, but the people who sent him down from Springfield figured he was on a one-way trip. It was known by the Beale Security Agency that Peters was unmarried, had no family. He came cheap. They paid him $1.14 a day to guard warehouses, banks, after hours; work funerals; ride shotgun on freight wagons. Like today.

Of course Duane Beale, owner of the agency, hoped Peters would make it through alive.

But of all his men, Peters was the most expendable.

He rode on the front seat of the box wagon, a Rider No. 2 rolling-block .44 rifle across his lap. His hand caressed the fishbelly buttstock as the wagon, driven by Walt Dover, rattled along the trail that coursed up Turkey Creek, out of Hollister, Missouri. Peters wore a Remington .44 pistol high on his gunbelt, which was more comfortable but not easy to reach from a sitting position. He was a short, bow-legged man, with a bushy handlebar mustache, wide sideburns, close-set eyes, and a thin nose. His mean little lips were concealed under the whiskers.

Dover, a man in his fifties, flinched every time the 24-inch barrel of the Remington Rider poked him in the side. He chewed on a thick cud of tobacco, spoke at lickety-split, half of his words drowned out by the clatter of the paired team's hooves on the stoney ground.

"This warn't nothin' but a trail once't," chattered Dover, "rid only by the post rider. Nearest post office was in Springfield. That 'uz back in '34, 'fore yore time. I run the mail down from Springfield to Carrolton, then drive a stagecoach as far as the ferry. We alluz stopped there in Kirbyville to take on passengers, pick up the post, and such."

Peters heard half of Dover's talk.

"How far to the ferry?"

"A piece yet. That's when it'll happen, after we cross the White."

"Damn it, what're you talking about, old man?"

"Expectin' trouble, ain't ye?"

"Maybe."

Beale had told him to expect trouble. Beale hadn't told him that they would pick up three riders on the other side of the White River, specially picked sharpshooters, ordered to stay back of the dust spooled up by the box wagon. Within a rifle shot's distance. The three men had stayed in Hollister, Missouri, the night before; had crossed over on the ferry early that morning.

"You know them boys is pretty smart," cackled the old man.

"What boys is that?"

"Them what's robbin' all the payrolls down to Lead Hill in Arkansas. The stagecoaches. Mighty bold bunch, you ask me."

"Jesus, just keep us on the road."

The wagon hurtled a corner in the road on two wheels. Peters hung on to keep from falling off the seat.

"Don't want to miss the ferry." Dover pulled out a battered pocket watch, held it up for a long time as it bounced up and down, blurring the numbers on its face. "Shouldna stopped back there in Hollister."

"I was thirsty."

Peters had ordered Dover to pull up to the Red Lion, a tavern, where he'd bought a pail of beer. The ride down from Springfield had been hot and dusty, and his nerves were jangling like a sackful of washers. The beer gave him the edge he wanted. His butt was as sore as a boil, and Dover's incessant chatter had filed off the little that remained of his tolerance. Beale had said the wagon was carrying important papers, nothing that a red-legged robber would be interested in, for sure.

Peters didn't know it, but Duane Beale had lied.

The pouch in the back of the wagon contained three thousand dollars in cash. It was deliverable to an agent in Carrolton, Arkansas, who would turn over a valuable load of wild ginseng root to be shipped to China out of San Francisco. Ginseng was thought to have aphrodisiacal properties by the Chinese. Beale thought an unscheduled freighter

might have a chance of getting through. The robbers, however, had not missed much the past few months. For added
security, Beale came up with the idea of having the sharpshooters tail the wagon once it crossed the White River and
headed for the Arkansas border.

Atop one of the hills, Dover pointed out yet another
landmark.

"Gobbler's Knob," he said. "That bald spot. Yonder is
Pine Top, south of there. Glad we ain't goin' that way along
Pine Top Road. Yessir, there's some rock outcroppings
down there what gives me the shiverin' shakes. Bushwhackers used it during the war and still do. They call them
rocks Murder Rocks now. Favorite place of old Alf Bolin."

Peters knew of Bolin, a notorious outlaw that the vigi-
lante group known as the Baldknobbers helped capture. He
shuddered, thinking of what had happened to Bolin. They
had beheaded him, shown his lifeless head around, then
threw it to the hogs.

A flock of merino sheep grazed on the bluestem grass
south of Kirbyville, lifting their heads as the wagon passed,
looking like gumless old men chewing meat. Some, on the
road, flowed over the knobby knoll as Dover cracked his
whip.

"Damned sheep," he muttered.

Peters looked out over the rolling countryside, ahead to
the thick woods. He licked his lips, felt a sudden pang of
apprehension. Between here and Blackwell's Ferry the
country was sparsely populated. He felt uncomfortable, even
though he knew that the highwaymen always struck along
the Missouri-Arkansas border.

But sometimes a man will feel things in his gut, in his
heart, that don't make much sense at first. Peters tried to
shake off the feeling that something was not quite right.

Dover's endless chatter now seemed to rise in pitch, skirt the edges of hysteria.

"Shut up, Walt!" he said suddenly, without reason.

"Huh?"

But Dover turned silent, and now the only sound was the creak of the wagon on its springs, the rattle of leather traces, the clodding footfalls of the horses. They passed by the little settlement of Mildred without stopping and began the slow descent through the hills to the river.

The road wound into the woods, following the natural contour of the ridge.

"Whatsamatter, Peters?"

"I dunno. Just shut your trap."

Peters loosened his pistol in his holster. He moved the rifle, setting it on its butt between his legs.

"'Bout time you took that damned thing out of my ribs," snapped Dover.

The road took them through the thick pinewoods. A deer jumped out of the brush ahead of them and bounded across the road. Peters flinched and brought the rifle up to a foot off the floor of the wagon.

"A mite spooky, ain't ye, Peters?"

Peters let out a breath.

"A mite."

"Why, this road's plumb peaceable. You get close to the border and you kin start frettin'."

But no sooner had Dover said these words when a rider appeared out of the trees just ahead. He stopped his big Tennessee walker square in the middle of the road. Dover hauled in on the reins.

Peters pulled the rifle up waist-high.

Suddenly more riders broke from cover, coming alongside the wagon. All had rifles. All the rifles were aimed at the two men in the wagon.

"Just bring her to a slow stop," drawled one of the men on horseback. "And you put that rifle away real slow, mister."

Peters had his orders.

If he was covered and outnumbered, he was not to try to shoot it out.

He put down the rifle.

The wagon jolted to a stop a few yards away from the man who blocked their way. He maneuvered his walker up between the team and the wagon. He was a tall man, square-shouldered, with a lean, hawk-faced look, deep sunk dark eyes, a hooked nose, a thick beard, and big, sensuous lips. He wore a battered Confederate campaign hat, and gray shirt and trousers. His boots were red, rough-outs, like those of the others. He sat his horse with a military bearing. His pistol was concealed in an Army holster, worn cross-draw fashion. The embossed initials, CSA, stood out on the flap. His Spencer carbine didn't waver a fraction of an inch from side to side as he leveled it at Peters.

"You, driver," said the leader. "Throw out that satchel goin' to Carrolton."

Peters frowned.

Dover reached behind him into the wagon.

"Slow. Don't bring nothin' out, 'ceptin' that satchel."

Dover's hand grasped the money pouch and drew it out of the wagon slowly.

"Just drop it on the ground."

The driver let the bag drop. It landed with a *whop!* The other riders held steady, their horses well-disciplined.

"Old man," said the leader. "You just sit plumb and nobody's gonna hurt you. Hobie, you shake out some rope for the Pinkerton."

Peters felt something inside him go pitch dark. A hard

lead ball formed in his stomach and began to grow. Two weeks ago a Pinkerton operative had been found swinging from the bridge in Alpena, Arkansas. He had a note pinned to his chest. The news traveled as far as Kansas City, and the Springfield paper carried the story. The note had read: "Death to Yankee Detectives." The Pinkertwon man who was killed was named Tom Silby, and he was from Chicago.

"I ain't no Pinkerton," said Peters. "I just work for Beale."

Hobart Stamper, the one called Hobie, rode up close, uncoiling a lariat that had seen some use. To Peters, the rope looked like a live snake in his hands.

"Take his pistol first," said the man on the Walker. "Don't give him no temptation."

Hobie leaned over the wagon and deftly plucked the pistol from the guard's holster. He tossed it to the man giving the orders, who caught it by the butt and shoved it in his waist-band.

"Get down," said Hobart. He was a thick-necked, pig-eyed man, with sloping brute shoulders and a small mouth. His hair, thick and unruly, jutted from under a battered peak-crowned black hat. His face was bushy with beard.

"You're making a hell of a mistake," said Peters. "I told you, I—"

"Shut up," said the man on the Tennessee horse.

Peters climbed down. The dark inside him turned cold. He looked at the blue sky, the trees. His eyes flickered with something like pain, but it was deeper than that, more elusive, less tangible. Maybe he would have called it sorrow, or regret.

Hobart shook out the loop, twirled it only once. The rope, like a snake's shadow, dropped over Peters. Hobart jerked it up tight around his chest and looped the slack end around his saddle horn. He whacked his horse on the rump and dug small, wicked spurs into the animal's flanks.

The horse bolted away. Peters, jerked off his feet, saw the ground rush up to meet him.

He hit the ground with a brain-jarring thud. A chorus of yells from the outlaws shattered his ears. Rock and grit smashed into his face, blinding him. His arms, pinned to his sides, were useless. He felt himself being bounced along, pain shooting through his kneecaps, his shoulders. The horse picked up speed, and Peters felt fresh blood course down his cheek. He tried holding his head up, but the pain jolted him senseless. His face struck a large rock, and his cheekbone shattered. He opened his mouth to scream, but there was nothing in his throat but a scratchy husk.

Old man Dover watched Peters being dragged away.

"You tell Beale we don't like Pinkertons," said the leader.

"Yes sir Mr. Mantooth, I——I shorely will," stuttered Dover.

Seth Mantooth's eyes narrowed.

"You better forget my name too, Dover, you know what's good for you."

"Yes, I done forgot it."

Dover heard Peters scream once.

Then it was quiet.

CHAPTER TWO

The Harrison Cartage Company had a building on First Street in Springfield. The Beale Security Agency shared the same building. The offices were in front, the loading docks in back. Duane Beale stood on the loading dock, a stub of a pencil in his hand, a pair more stuck in his shirt pocket. A sheaf of bills of lading lay on a large crate he used for a stand-up desk. He was of medium height and stood on a small wooden box so he could see over the crate as the loading continued. He had sandy hair and bulging blue eyes, the whites of which were streaked with red. His bulbous nose was lined with veiny blue protrusions, pus-filled lumps. He was corpulent, thick-lipped. His breath reeked of whiskey.

"Godamn it, Mike, get that wagon loaded and away from the dock," he said. "We've got 'em stacked up here."

Mike O'Malley, the dock foreman, stank of sweat. His chambray shirt was stuck to his massive back. The drays

9

were lined up, waiting to load, their drivers smoking, exchanging small talk.

"Now what?" asked Beale as a wagon lumbered up the alley, crowded between the drays. The mule shouldered its way past the waiting wagons and stopped at the dock.

"Hell, I don't know. Mister," said Mike. "Get your damned mule out of here. This is a private loading dock."

Beale scowled as he looked at the gaudy lettering on the side of the small Studebaker wagon. His nose wrinkled as he determined that the dandy holding the reins was an itinerant apothecary, obviously come to peddle his homeopathic medicines, nostrums, health restorers, invigorators, and the like. The co-owner of the freight company walked to the edge of the dock, arms akimbo, face swelled up with a blushing rage.

He glared down at a man dressed more in keeping with St. Louis high society than with the working class of Springfield, Missouri. The medicine drummer wore a tricot long suit, complementary vest, immaculate silk shirt, five-button Melton overgaiters, and a pearl gray derby with a curly brim. A smoking cheroot jutted pugnaciously from his mouth.

"Whoa there, Judith," said the man as he reached for the brake.

"You just turn that wagon around and be about your business some other place," ordered Beale.

"On the contrary," said the man, "I have important business here. Are you Duane Augustus Beale?"

Beale cringed at the full reading of his name.

"What of it?"

The apothecary reached inside his coat and pulled forth a sheaf of documents.

At that moment, three men on horseback rode up from behind the Studebaker.

"Uh oh," said Mike. "It's the damned sheriff."

"And," said the man in the derby hat, "two deputies."

Beale stepped forward on the dock and squinted.

"Edwin? What's all the commotion? You know this jasper?"

Sheriff Edwin Wales, his ruddy face specked with freckles, cracked an apologetic smile.

"Feller here has some business with you what can't wait," he said.

"You have to bring Bob and Hal with you?" He cocked a thumb toward the pair of deputies, Hal Meadows and Bob Smith. "You ain't fixin' to arrest anyone, are you?"

Wales looked sheepish as he shook his head.

"We better talk inside. Be a while, so you just as well tell these drovers to come back later."

"Damn it, Edwin, I got work to do here."

The man in the Studebaker set the brake and wrapped the reins around the handle. He climbed up on the dock. He had weight to him but wasn't fat, not by a long shot. His clear blue eyes shimmered with an intense light. He handed the papers in his hand to Beale.

Beale read them over.

Mike started to walk away.

"You stay here, Mike," said Wales, dismounting. He wrapped his reins around a snubbing post and climbed the stairs to the dock. He took off his hat and wiped sweat from the band. The deputies made sure the drovers moved their wagons, then went away.

Beale cursed again and glared at the man in the derby with undisguised annoyance.

"What's all this mean?" asked Beale. "This looks like a search warrant. What you searching for?"

"We'll talk about that inside."

"You a marshal or something?"

"Pinkerton. The name's Weatherbee. Doc Weatherbee."

Beale laughed out loud.

"You? A Pinkerton agent?"

"We call ourseles operatives."

"You look more like a damned medicine drummer."

Doc took Beale's arm and ushered him through the back door of the freight office. His grasp was firm, his strength evident in the hardness of his grip. Beale tried to shake him off, but Weatherbee tightened his hold until Beale winced.

They went through a storage area and down a hallway to the main offices. A girl with red hair looked up from her desk. She had a pen in hand and was entering figures into a ledger book. The girl was very pretty. Her eyebrows lifted when she saw Doc's hand on Beale's arm. Walt Dover, seated on the other side of the counter, coughed self-consciously. The sun streamed through the big glass window, sending mote-filled columns of light into the office, past the big black block letters that read: HARRISON CARTAGE COMPANY and BEALE SECURITY AGENCY. There were three other men seated on the bench opposite Dover, each one hard-faced, lean, flint-eyed.

"Wh-what are you doing here, Dover?" gasped Beale.

"Which one is your office, Beale?" asked Weatherbee.

Beale pointed to a closed door.

"We'll talk in there," said the Pinkerton.

The men crowded into Beale's office.

"Sit down," ordered Weatherbee.

Beale sat down behind a large, paper-cluttered desk. Spindled papers were spiked onto long nails driven through one-inch blocks. A grimy calendar with a bathing-suit clad woman hung on the wall, along with various charts and maps of the trails that laced the region. A large slate chalkboard on the wall kept track of the agents and their assigned wagons. Wales leaned against the wall, next to the calendar. His deputies stood at the ready on either side of the door.

Mike O'Malley stood in a corner behind his boss. Doc sat on the desk, swinging his leg idly. He drew deep on his cheroot and picked a few flecks of lint from his coat.

"Now," he said softly, "some questions. Two weeks ago a man was killed. Name of Peters. He worked for you. You lost a satchel containing three thousand dollars. That right?"

"Right," said Beale.

"Dover out there—he drove the wagon that day?"

"You know damned well he did."

"He says the robbers believed Peters was a Pinkerton."

"Hell, how would I know?"

Doc's jaw hardened, twitched with a flickering muscle.

"Dover didn't know he was heading into a trap. He said Peters didn't know he was carrying hard cash."

"What's the point, Weatherbee?"

"You set Peters up."

"Like hell I did!"

Doc's face wrinkled in a look of disgust. He looked at the sheriff and nodded.

Wales cleared his throat.

"This is a pretty serious charge, Duane," said Wales. "This feller got a judge out of bed to issue a search warrant and something else."

"What's that?"

"An open arrest warrant. If you don't answer this Pinkerton's questions right, I got to take you to jail."

"Shit," said Beale. He drove a fist into the desk top, rattling a pile of papers. "What do you want to know, Weatherbee?"

"First, why'd you hire those three gunnies out there?"

"Figured we could jump the robbers if they tried to hold up Dover and Peters."

Doc's features twisted into a disbelieving frown. He stopped swinging his leg. He mashed out the stub of his

Old Virginia cheroot in a clay ashtray. He fixed Beale with a piercing stare.

"Let's cut out all the nonsense, Beale," he said, "and get down to brass tacks. You knew that Peters was going to get ambushed. Trouble was, you had your hired gunnies on the wrong side of the river. A man got killed, and the bandits thought he was a Pinkerton operative."

"Well, he wasn't, so I don't see why you've got anything to say about this."

"You dumb mule. If they thought he was a Pinkerton and killed him anyway, that means we *are* in it. They've already killed one of our men."

"Peters knew what he was in for. He was armed."

"No, he didn't know what he was facing, Beale. If he had, he might be alive today. You didn't tell him he was carrying money, and you didn't tell him you figured he'd be ambushed."

Beale drew in a deep breath and blew it out through his nostrils. He doubled and undoubled one of his fists. Sheriff Wales looked at him with a pitying look.

"All right. I thought we could get away with it," admitted Beale. "I didn't want to tell Peters because the word might get out. I didn't know he'd get ambushed. At least not on that side of the river. I hired those three hardcases to follow Dover after he took the ferry across. They've never hit on this side of the border before."

Doc let out a breath.

"Now we're getting somewhere," he said. "There was a leak somewhere. On your end. I don't think Dover knew what he was carrying."

"No."

"Who else besides you knew about the money?"

"Why, nobody. Except Paul Stone, who owns Harrison

Cartage. Even Mike here didn't know what was in that satchel."

"Nobody? Come on, Beale. Those robbers knew what Dover was carrying."

Beale's forehead wrinkled up in thought.

Doc pressed him.

"Who's Seth Mantooth? Dover said he knew him."

"I don't know. He used to ride with Quantrill. A damned redleg. An Arky. Pure mean."

"Think Dover found out about the money?"

"No. The bill of lading said only that he was carrying documents. I had Molly out there fill them out."

"Molly the redhead?"

"Yeah. Molly Clemson. She's..."

Doc was off the desk in a flash. He pulled open the door and rushed into the outer office.

The redhead was gone.

"Dover?" Doc shouted. "Where'd the girl go?"

Walt Dover's eyes went wide.

"She—she was listening at that door there a minute ago."

Doc whirled and raced out back. He heard pounding hoofbeats. The sheriff's horse was missing. He ran down the stairs and looked up the alley. The girl, her red hair flying, was riding away at full gallop. Doc patted his waistband, but he knew he wasn't carrying his pistol. He had left it in the wagon. He considered chasing after her on one of the deputies' horses, but she turned the corner and disappeared. He muttered something under his breath and stalked back up the stairs. The girl could ride, he thought.

Wales was standing in the doorway of Beale's office when Doc returned.

"Run out on you, did she?"

"That appears to be the case. Step aside, Wales. I've got

some more questions to ask Beale."

Beale wore a smirk on his face.

"What'd you do, Weatherbee, scare off my office help?"

"It's not funny, Beale. That girl knew something. She was eavesdropping on our conversation. How long has she been working for you?"

"About two months. Best gal we ever had. She works for Stone, too."

"Tell me all about it. Why you hired her, when you hired her, and who worked at her desk before she did."

"Not much to tell. We had a gal out there who didn't show up one day. I was going to put out a notice when this Molly Clemson comes up looking for a job. I seen she knew how to read and write, so I put her to work."

"Where's she from?"

"Hell, I don't know. Said she lived over to Mae Scaggs' boardinghouse. She was clean, didn't say much."

"So you told her you were sending three thousand dollars down to Arkansas?"

"Sure did. She had to know what Stone was shipping," drawled Beale.

"She knew dates, times, and contents of all shipments."

"Damn, Doc, you're thick in the head, ain't you? Molly was the shipping clerk. Her and Mike knew what come in, what went out."

"Where's Stone anyway?" asked Doc.

"Out of town," said O'Malley. "He spends half the time in Harrison, half here. I'm in charge when he's gone. Me and Duane."

Doc looked at Mike.

"You ever see that woman before she worked here?"

The Irish youth shook his head.

Doc looked at one of the deputies.

"You, Meadows?"

"I'm Smith."

"Go fetch Dover. Bring him in here. Maybe he knows something."

Bob Smith opened the door.

Just as he did so, an explosion blew in the front window of the office. Smith hurtled backwards and crashed against the doorjamb. The windows rattled. Calendars shook on the walls. A framed business license hit the floor. Doc was knocked off his feet by the force of the blast. Smoke and dust billowed into the room.

O'Malley, Wales, and Meadows braced themselves against the shaking walls.

Doc scrambled to his feet. Gasping and choking, he struggled through the smoke in the outer office.

Plaster from the shattered walls lay strewn on the floor. The front windows were blown in. Shards of broken glass lay on the counter. Doc lifted the hinged part of the counter and walked through the opening. He dreaded what he might see.

Four men lay dead on the floor. Dover, his neck broken, his face bleeding, stared up at him with sightless eyes. The three gunmen lay in a twisted heap of smoking flesh. Their clothes were ripped to shreds. Pieces of flesh stuck against the counter, the walls. The stench of death mingled with the acrid tang of dynamite.

Wales and the others came up behind Doc.

"Christ almighty," said the sheriff. "Blown all to hell."

Beale's face twisted into a mask of fear.

Mike O'Malley started to get sick.

Hal Meadows' face blanched and turned ashen.

The shaken Bob Smith hung groggily on to the counter.

A crowd started to gather outside the building.

The smoke settled.

Doc Weatherbook shook his head and stepped outside for air. He knew before he asked the question what the answer would be.

Nobody saw anything.

Four men dead, and the killers got away scot-free.

Slowly, Doc's anger started to build.

CHAPTER THREE

Raider started changing his identity in St. Louis.

His instructions from Allan Pinkerton, by way of Wagner in Chicago, were clear.

> MEET WEATHERBEE SPRINGFIELD STOP MAGNOLIA
> HOTEL STOP WALNUT STREET STOP YOU ARE ARKAN-
> SAS MAN STOP GO VIA FREIGHT WAGON STOP DEPART
> ST. LOUIS THIS DATE STOP UTMOST SECRECY STOP
> ALLAN EXPRESSLY PICKED YOU FOR THIS ONE STOP
> WAGNER

The first thing Raider did after receiving his orders was to forget to shave. The next thing he did was to get mad as hell. He got mad at Allan Pinkerton and he got mad at Wagner. Then he got mad at the schedule, and at schedules in general.

Finally he got mad at the mode of transportation Wagner had ordered him to take. He knew the country where he was headed. The rugged Ozarks, with their endless hills and their thick-brushed hollows, could take the starch out of a hurrying man, give him a fear of being closed in, blocked off, shut out, and in a kind of prison with green trees for walls.

He knew the White River Valley south of Springfield, knew its history. He also knew there was a train now from St. Louis to Springfield. Yet Wagner had ordered him to go by freight wagon. Why?

He was sure he could revert back to his Arkansas heritage. He was, after all, from Viola, down in Fulton County. He had been with the Pinkerton National Detective Agency for seven years, and the memory of his roots was not that far away from him.

Raider, who stood a strapping six foot two in his stockinged feet, was tough as rawhide from years in the saddle. His tanned, sun-weathered face framed dark flinty eyes. He made a striking figure with his jet-black hair and mustache as he strode into a secondhand store and bought farm boy's cast off clothes and old farmer's boots to go with his new image. He packed away his black Stetson, his denims, his disreputable-looking leather jacket, his calfskin Middleton boots. He shipped the trunk to Springfield via the St. Louis–San Francisco Railroad. He carried his pistol, a converted Remington .44, in a moth-eaten carpetbag. His rifle went with him, rolled up in an equally ragged blanket.

"Where you bound, friend?" asked Raider when he went to the yards where the freighters were outfitting. He knew damned well where they were going, because he had asked at the right places. The man he spoke to looked up from the bales of cotton already loaded on the flatbed rig. He regarded Raider with a friendly eye.

"Springfield."

"I'm a-goin' there myself."

"Need a ride?"

"Sure do."

"Well grab aholt of a cotton bale and let's get her loaded. If you can drive a team, the widder Melton and her daughter, Ginger, need a drover."

"I can handle a team."

Raider grinned. His clothes and his accent had evidently passed muster. He still didn't feel comfortable with his slow Arkansas drawl, buried for so many years now, but he knew it would come back with time. Perhaps Allan Pinkerton was smart enough to know that and that's why he had ordered Raider to go south with the wagons.

"When you leaving?" he asked later.

"Soon's we're loaded. They's five others, including the widder and her daughter, a-goin' with us."

The man, a cadaverous lanky fellow in his forties, with a grizzled beard and a peaked hat, shoved a hand in Raider's face.

"My name's Ruben Boggs. I hail from Fairview, down in Arkansas."

"Name's Raider. I'm From Viola."

"You been away?"

"Awhile."

"Thought so. Your hands don't have no plow calluses."

Raider looked self-consciously at his hands. The palms were smooth.

"I'll get back to it," he said.

The two men worked fast and easy. Soon they had the wagon loaded. Other wagons, carrying a variety of goods, pulled up and formed into a train. Evidently Boggs was the wagonmaster, because they all lined up behind his rig. The wagons carried household goods, cotton, chickens, farm equipment. There were some women along, no small children. Raider didn't know whether the freighters were for hire or if these were just immigrants moving south.

"Widder's wagon is over behind that shed there," said Boggs, pointing. "Jest interduce yourself and drive that team up to the rear."

"Glad to," said Raider, picking up his gear.

Behind the shed stood a wagon similar to the others, with a team of horses hitched to its singletree. Two women were struggling with the bows. Raider set down his luggage and strode over to them.

"Give you a hand," he said. The bows were removable, fit into hoops on the sides of the wagon box. A heavy, waterproof sheet of canvas, or duck, could be drawn tightly over the bows to protect the cargo from rain, snow, or the hot sun. Raider set the bows and pulled the sheet up tight to make a covered wagon.

"Thank you, mister. Much obliged," said the older of the two women.

"Welcome, ma'am," said Raider politely. He doffed the battered hat he wore. "I reckon I'm your driver to Springfield. The name's Raider."

"Why, Mr. Raider, how nice," said the woman. "I'm Grace Melton. This is my daughter Ginger."

He looked at them closely for the first time. They looked more like sisters than mother and daughter. Grace was a comely woman with fine light hair, hazel eyes, a stern tapering nose, and full lips. She wore no rouge on her cheeks, and the bonnet on her head covered most of her hair. Ginger was a smaller, leaner version of her mother, with greenish-tinted hazel eyes, a shorter nose that was every bit as slender, even riper lips, and a bodice that bulged like a sackful of melons.

"Pleased to meet you, ladies," said Raider.

The women exchanged glances and flickering smiles. Raider threw his gear up in the back of the wagon as they watched him.

"Are you from around here?" asked Ginger. She had a soft, musical voice, accented with that Arkansas drawl he knew so well.

"From down to Viola," he said.

"Why, we're from Berryville," said Ginger, her voice plaintive, as though she were singing. "Going back home now that Ma's widdered so young and all."

"Sorry, ma'am."

"Ginger, come along now," said her mother. "We don't want to talk about unpleasant things to a stranger."

Raider was relieved.

The widow wore black, but her daughter was dressed in a gay gingham dress that accented the curves of her hips. When he helped them up, they both showed fine trim ankles.

"You from St. Louis?" he asked.

"My husband lived there," said Grace. "Owned a store. His heart give out, poor man. We sold everything so's we could go back to Berryville. St. Louis is too fast a town for a couple of country girls."

Ginger giggled.

Raider climbed up on the seat and unwrapped the reins from around the brake. Ginger sat next to him, in the middle, her thigh pressing against his own.

He clucked to the team and rattled the reins.

The horses moved.

"Why, you handle this team right smartly," said Grace, smiling broadly.

"Thank you, ma'am," said Raider, noting that his Arkansas drawl was getting more perfect all the time.

"You sure do," said Ginger. "I think we're going to have a fine trip, Ma."

"We surely will," said Mrs. Melton.

Raider was looking forward to it as Ginger leaned against him on the turn around the shed.

*   *   *

The land was rugged. So were the teamsters who wrestled the wagons over hard roads, through mire and mud, over hills, across streams. Raider soon found that he had his work cut out for him. Boggs, it turned out, was a hard taskmaster, one of the breed of men who not only built the roads but tamed them through a fierce determination.

When they stopped, that first night, Raider wondered if there was any bone in his body that didn't ache. The women seemed to take the jolting better than he, for they cheerfully took to helping set up camp and get the cook fires started. After he put up the team for the night, hobbling the horses so they wouldn't stray far, he soaked in a stream and let the wind dry him as he lay exhausted next to a log. Drowsy, he dozed until Ginger shook him.

He smelled her musk, her perfume, looked up into her green eyes.

"Time to eat supper," she said.

Raider groaned.

"Come on. We can eat together. I made biscuits especially for you."

Her hand brushed across his face. He felt a stirring in his loins.

He looked around to see if anyone was watching. The fire blazed high, and people were busy ladling food into tin plates.

"Ginger, you make a man mighty hungry."

She laughed low in her throat.

"First you get something to eat."

Suppertime was laced with lighthearted banter. Raider sat with Ginger and her mother. He spoke but little. The talk was mostly about how the land was changing, the James boys, the Daltons and the Youngers, all familiar to those who traveled through Missouri and Arkansas.

After supper, Boggs came up to Raider and offered him a smoke. Raider shook his head.

"Want you to take the first watch," said Boggs. "I'll have a man relieve you at midnight."

"You expect trouble?"

"Some of the women are a might techy, what with the talk about the James bunch. These roads do attract thieves. You have a gun?"

"I reckon so."

"Just keep your eyes open and your ears perked."

Raider shook out his bedroll and spread his blankets under the widow Melton's wagon. The women had made their beds in the box, under canvas. He unpacked his rifle and strapped on his pistol.

"Good night, Mrs. Melton," he said.

"Good night."

"Just a minute. I'll walk a ways with you," said Ginger.

Raider looked at Grace, who turned away quickly. Her daughter smiled ingenuously and followed after him. When they were out of earshot of her mother, she stopped him with a hand on his arm and stood on tiptoe.

"Don't shoot me if I come to see you after everyone's asleep," she said.

"Ginger, you better get some sleep. We've got a long day tomorrow."

Impulsively, she put her arms around his neck and pulled herself up, her body pressing against his. She kissed him on the mouth. Before he could say anything, she ran away, back to her wagon.

"Damn fool gal," he muttered. But her kiss burned on his lips, and he couldn't forget her breasts mashing against his chest.

The camp settled down. It grew quiet. Raider walked a wide circle and found a spot to sit that gave him a high view of the camp. There was a low, natural rock wall, a jumble of rocks where he could stand or sit. Stars sprinkled the skies; they twinkled silently like the far lights of a town.

Somewhere a wolf howled and a farm dog yapped a brave reply before it, too, turned silent.

An hour went by. Raider believed that everyone was fast asleep. However, as he looked down at the shadowy shapes of the camp, a white-clad figure detached itself from the dark silhouette of a wagon and headed his way up the gentle slope. He stood up, rifle at the ready.

"Raider," said a soft voice. "Don't shoot."

He set his rifle down as Ginger loomed larger in the darkness. She wore a white gown and sandals. She carried rolled-up blankets under her arm.

"Ginger, what . . . ?"

"Shhh!" she whispered. "You'll wake up the whole camp."

"What in hell are you doing here?"

"I came to be with you, silly."

"I'm on guard."

"Boggs probably put you out here on purpose."

"Huh?"

"To keep us apart. He's sweet on me."

"You've got some imagination, little lady."

She laid out the blankets, putting them behind the rock wall.

"I've seen the way he looks at me."

"You're pretty bold," he said.

"And lonesome."

"Ginger, if Boggs or your ma catches you up here, my ass is mud."

"So lie down with me. Keep me warm."

She cuddled up to him and embraced him around the

neck. Her scent was thick in his nostrils, a cloying perfume that made him giddy with desire. Her breasts pressed into his chest. Again she kissed him. This time her tongue slithered inside his mouth. He found himself responding to her kiss, ignoring the warning klaxon sounding in his brain.

Raider had been without a woman for over a week. This was unusual for him, but the Pinkertons had kept him busy. Now he was here with a willing woman. It was dark and they were alone.

She pulled him onto the blankets. He grabbed her and drew her to him. Her hand found the bulge between his legs and began to rub the knotted hardness.

"Ginger," he breathed. "You're plumb loco."

"I know. I couldn't breathe when you sat next to me all day. I wanted to get you in the back of the wagon. I wanted you bad."

"What would your ma say?"

"She'd wish she was me."

Raider drew back in surprise. Ginger's words had the ring of truth. He knew how hungry a woman could get, especially after she had lost her man.

Then he had no more time to think, as Ginger slipped out of her grown, offering her naked body to his.

"Hurry," she husked, her fingers plucking at his clothes. "I'm on fire."

Raider stripped quickly and moved over her body.

Her hand reached for him, grabbed the swollen hardness.

In the starlit dark, she was beautiful.

Raider wanted her, and he didn't give a damn about the consequences.

CHAPTER FOUR

The wagon train pulled into Springfield late in the afternoon. Raider learned that Springfield had two wagon yards where the freighters made their headquarters. One was called the Missouri Yard. Boggs pulled into the Arkansas Yard, since he planned to go on into that state after unloading his cotton and other goods.

Raider chuckled when he saw the large sign erected at the entrance. The sign consisted of poles connected by cross braces. On the top rail someone had nailed small boards together in the shape of an R, followed by a nailed-up oil can, which in turn was followed by a cross-cut saw hung from the top rail. Under these, the word "Yard" was made out of nailed-up boards. Thus the sign read: "R-Can-Saw Yard."

Raider helped unload the cotton bales and saw to it that the women were quartered away from the teamsters. He said his goodbye to Boggs.

"Been a pleasure, Raider," said the wagonmaster. "Anytime you want to haul freight, you look me up."

"I'll do that."

It was harder to say farewell to Grace and Ginger Melton.

"Oh, can't you go with us to Berryville?" wailed Ginger.

"No, I have business here in Springfield."

"But—"

"Now, now, child," said her mother. "Don't make Mr. Raider feel bad. You say goodbye and then run along. I want to speak private to our benefactor."

Ginger pouted, but she knew better than to openly disobey her mother. She said goodbye as tears brimmed up in her eyes. Then, impulsively, she stood up on tiptoe and kissed him on the cheek.

Raider, hat in hand, watched Ginger walk away. Her mother stepped in close.

"I hope you *will* visit us down to Berryville real soon," she said.

"I'll try and do that, ma'am."

"We'll be easy to find. The Meltons own considerable property down there. My husband's pa has graciously given us a small farm where we hope to settle and start a new life."

Raider shifted his weight, anxious to be off.

"Yes'm."

"I hope you enjoyed yourself with my daughter."

"Huh?"

"Oh, I'm well aware of Ginger's ways. She's right smartly attracted to you. I don't put much blame on her, poor dear. I find my own heart all aflutter at this very moment."

Raider swallowed.

"Ma'am, I reckon I just better say goodbye and take my leave."

She leaned close to him and put her hand on his.

"Just remember, if you come down our way, that while

I may be a widow, I'm alive. And I'm a woman, too."

"Yes'm," said Raider. "You sure as hell are, ma'am."

She kissed him then, and he felt the fire in her lips. It was not a peck, but a lingering kiss that made his flesh tingle.

For a long moment he considered not leaving at all just then, but Grace broke the kiss and turned away.

"Goodbye," she choked.

"Wait a minute," he said. "You never told me how your husband died."

She turned and fixed him with a sharp look. Her face twisted up, and she drew her lips together tightly.

"Why, he was hanged, Mr. Raider. Didn't Ginger tell you?"

"No," he rasped. "Why?"

"He was a thief," she said softly.

Before he could say anything more, she was gone, back to the wagon where Ginger waited, sobbing quietly to herself.

Raider put his hat on and stalked out of the yard. He got a ride into town with one of the teamsters who was going after whiskey. The man was half drunk and didn't say much on the ride in to town. But he knew where the Magnolia Hotel was and let Raider out right at its doorstep.

The Pinkerton checked in and found he had a message waiting for him.

"You're in room seven; turn left at the top of the stairs," said the clerk.

Raider opened the envelope and read the message.

"Meet me at Frenchy's," it read. "8:00 P.M." It was signed simply, "Doc."

"How long's this message been here?" asked Raider.

"Two, three days."

"The man who left it. He staying here?"

"Room four." The clerk didn't even look up.

"Where's Frenchy's?"

The clerk started to laugh, until he looked into Raider's eyes.

"Second and Main. Hell, I thought everybody knew where Frenchy's was."

"What is it, a whorehouse?"

This time the clerk did laugh.

"It's got a little bit of everything. Maybe you been there already and just don't remember it."

Raider stalked upstairs to his room. He threw his rifle, blanket, and carpetbag on the bed, then walked down the hall to number four. He knocked softly. There was no answer.

Back in his room, Raider lit an oil lamp and looked in the mirror. His beard was thick on his face now. Needed trimming. No one but his mother was likely to recognize him. He wondered what kind of a place Frenchy's was and why Doc wanted to meet him there. A public place wasn't exactly where two Pinkertons working undercover ought to be seen. He shrugged. Doc was peculiar, but he usually had good reasons for doing things.

Raider debated on whether or not to leave the pistol in his room. But he felt naked without it. He took everything out of the satchel except his .44 Remington. He looked, he thought, like a damned pilgrim. He turned down the lamp and watched it sputter and fume as the flame went out. He locked the door after he left, figuring it must be close to eight o'clock because of the way his gut was acting up. If he let it go too long, the pain would turn him inside out. There was something else, too. Raider hadn't had a drink in three weeks, and he had a powerful thirst.

* * *

The place wasn't named Frenchy's, Raider discovered. It was called La Maison de François.

For a long time people called it Frank Coy's, and then finally it just became Frenchy's. Although the French had controlled the great interior plains and low plateaus of the United States for almost a century and a half, they had left few footprints. It was almost as if they had never been there, and, except for the few place names in the Ozarks and their eighteenth-century houses at Ste. Geneviève, there were few reminders that they had once discovered, explored, and developed a vast region.

The establishment boasted an elaborate false front, all glittered up with silver and gold paint, figures of dancing girls, high kickers with scanty skirts and fishnet stockings. Raider walked up to the porch and looked through brightly lit windows. Oil lamps flickered on the walls. Men sat and talked at tables, under a pall of blue smoke, and glitter gals threaded their way between groups, smiling, flirting.

Raider went inside and made his way to the long bar with its brass rail and matching spittoons placed strategically every few feet. He ordered a whiskey from the bartender.

"Put your money down and I'll bring you a glass."

Raider threw a bill on the bar. The bartender examined it to see if it was genuine.

"Real trusting, ain't you?" said Raider.

"Mister, I've seen bank notes from every state of the Union and some what was made just down the street there. I don't trust nobody."

"Bring the whiskey."

The bartender scowled, but he poured Raider a drink, and he was generous.

"You want the bottle?"

"Just leave it. I have more money just as good as what you took."

Raider took a swallow of whiskey and turned around, his back to the bar. He saw no one he knew. A Waterbury on the wall said it was a little past eight o'clock. He was about to turn back around when he spotted a hand waving at him. Then he saw the pearl-gray derby with the curly brim. He waved back.

"I'll take the bottle," he said loudly.

"Three dollars," said the bartender.

Raider held it up. It was three-quarters full. Worth no more than two dollars if it was unopened.

He threw three cartwheels on the counter. He didn't stay to see the bartender bite each one, but grabbed the bottle and his glass and wended his way to Weatherbee's table.

"What kept you?" asked Doc when Raider came up to the table. There was a sarcastic tone to his voice.

"I didn't know I had to be here at any particular time.

"You got my note."

"No, I just come here all the time out of pure lonesomeness."

Doc pushed out a chair and gave Raider a dirty look.

"Sit down. I've got a lot to tell you."

"Shoot," said Raider.

"Poor choice of word."

Raider's eyebrows lifted. He worked with Doc Weatherbee but didn't particularly like his dandified ways. Doc had gone to Harvard; Raider had gone to an arbor school until he was eleven or twelve. The two men were poles apart, but they worked well together. And Raider knew that when the chips were down, when his life was on the line, Doc would be there, backing him up, steady as a blood brother.

"Better tell me what's going on," said Raider. "I feel like I've just wasted three weeks of time."

Doc suppressed a smile.

"I'd say you made the transition just fine. You look just like one of the kind of men we're after."

"What's that supposed to mean?"

Doc filled him in on all that had happened, all that he knew, from the hanging of the Pinkerton in Alpena to the murder of Peters and the dynamiting of the four men at the freight and security offices.

"I've been checking up on this Duane Beale," said Weatherbee. "I can't figure out if he's stupid, or shrewd as a fox."

"How so?"

"Four men, with direct connections to Beale, are now dead as doornails. And he's at least indirectly responsible for every one of them. He's hooked up with a man named Paul Stone who owns a freight company. From what I can determine, Stone's had fewer losses than some of the other outfits, but that last run cost him three thousand dollars."

"If Beale runs guards on the freighters, that's just smart business to have his setup in the same building."

Doc grimaced.

"That's just the trouble. It's too cozy. I brought those men up to confront Beale, let them talk in his presence. I sent them to their deaths."

"Don't take it so hard, Doc. It wasn't your fault."

"And that girl, Molly Clemson. I missed her completely. She got hired on without any questions being asked. She knew about the money being in that satchel. What do you say about that?"

"Handy," said Raider. "What about Mike O'Malley? He check out?"

"Yes. He seems not to have known about the money.

He works for Stone, but takes his orders from Beale when they load material going out under guard."

"So O'Malley must have known there was money or something valuable going out with Dover's wagon."

"No. He thought Peters was going along to guard the wagon on the return trip."

"Another dead end?"

"Maybe. Look, Raider, I've been too busy the last couple of days checking up on Beale. I still want to check out Mae Scaggs' boardinghouse and question the people there about the Clemson woman. Want to take it on?"

"I'm not doing anything," Raider drawled lazily.

"You will be. We've got to get inside that bunch down there. Springfield's a dead end, except for the woman. Beale's tightened up, and I can't get a thing out of him. I have a hunch that Molly Clemson was sent up here to spy on Harrison Cartage. Or maybe on Beale, if he's clean."

"You don't think he is?"

"I'll know pretty soon. Wagner's running a check on him. And any minute now that sheriff, Ed Wales, should be here with some more information on him and Seth Mantooth."

Raider looked around the room. He saw a number of drovers he had met on the Ridge Road down from St. Louis. Getting liquored up. Frenchy's, he decided, was quite a place. It had something for everyone. He wouldn't be surprised if there was a gambling room in the back. He had seen men coming and going through a door that was never left open; two men, both armed, stood on either side of it, checking on whoever wanted to go through. He had seen glitter gals going upstairs to the cribs more than once, the men following them like dogs after a bitch in heat.

Wales came alone.

"Sit down," said Doc. "Drink?"

The sheriff shook his head and looked at Raider, who said nothing. Nor did Weatherbee introduce the two men.

"What've you got, Wales?"

"Not much. Nothing on Beale to speak of. He was with Shelby's Iron Brigade, did some scouting, got into detective work after the war. He ain't married, but he lives with a woman. Nothing there. She doesn't read nor write, has nothing to do with Beale's business. Beale borrowed five hundred from the bank to start his agency, and he paid that back two years ago."

"He have any connection with Mantooth?"

"Maybe. I don't know."

"What does that mean?" asked Raider.

"You're digging deep into things best kept buried, mister."

"You better be plainer than that."

"Look, who are you anyway?"

"That's not important," said Doc quickly, hoping to avoid a flare of tempers. "He's with me."

"Well," said Wales, now testy as a hunting hound that's run up against a porcupine, "Beale served under Captain William Gregg who was with Shelby. So did Cole Younger, Dick Yager, and Frank James. Some of those boys also rode with Quantrill. Mantooth, for one. And Hobie Stamper, for another."

"Stamper is the only other name we have," explained Doc. "Dover told him that before he was killed."

Raider had heard of Quantrill, of course. Most everyone had.

"What are you saying, Wales?" asked Raider. "Exactly."

Wales swallowed and looked Raider straight in the eye.

"Maybe Beale rode with Quantrill too."

And there, thought both Doc and Raider, was the connection.

"There's one other thing I found out," said the sheriff, "but it's only talk, and I can't nail it down."

"We'll take it anyway," said Doc.

"Might not be a relative, might be. But there was one other name that come up as being with Selby and, later, with Quantrill."

"Who's that?" asked Weatherbee.

"A man named Norville Clemson."

"Well, I'll be damned," said Raider. "Sheriff, you done good."

CHAPTER FIVE

Doc lit an Old Virginia cheroot after the sheriff left Frenchy's, and ordered himself a brandy. Raider was just polishing off a thick steak, potatoes, and biscuits, washed down with scalding coffee. The desk clerk had been right. Frenchy's had just about everything a man could want or need.

"Ever heard of the jayhawkers, Raider?"

"I heard of 'em. Out of Kansas. During the war. Wore the red boots."

"Redlegs, they called them too."

"What about it?" Raider patted his belly. Most of the chronic pain had been smothered by the food he had eaten.

"Something Dover told me when I talked to him about this Mantooth character."

"Yeah?"

"He and his bunch wore those same kind of boots. And the robbery itself—it smacks of a military operation."

"What's the point, Doc?"

"Just this. There may be more to these robberies than meets the eye. From what I've learned, I'm getting a very ominous picture of that bunch."

"Whatever 'onimous' means."

"Ominous. Dire. Dark. Look, Raider, every posse that's gone after those redlegs comes back with reports of the robbers disappearing into thin air. Now that's not humanly possible. But it tells me that Mantooth is well organized. He hasn't made any mistakes."

Raider got up from the table and looked at Doc with narrowed eyes.

"He made one, Doc. He killed a man in cold blood that he thought was a Pinkerton."

"Yes. And he killed a Pinkerton as well. That's why Allan himself wants this boy real bad."

"We'll get him." Raider touched the brim of his battered hat. "See you, Doc."

"Where are you going?"

"To Skaggs' boardinghouse. I want to turn in early."

"Knock on my door when you get back. I should have word from Wagner by then."

Raider winked at Doc.

"Don't knock on my door. I may be busy." Raider's glance drifted to a glitter gal's behind as she passed by, bouncing her buttocks.

"Is that all you think about, Raider?"

"Same as you, Doc, same as you."

Raider walked away, leaving Doc with his mouth open, a brandy glass halfway to his lips. The disguised Pinkerton hugged a girl on the way out and whispered something in her ear.

Doc swallowed his brandy in one gulp, nearly gagging on the strong liquid.

When his eyes cleared of mist, Raider was gone.

* * *

Mrs. Skaggs' boardinghouse was within walking distance of the Magnolia Hotel. Raider didn't mind the stroll in the flat-heeled farmer's boots, but he missed having a horse under him.

The false fronts on Second Street gave way to modest frame houses, their windows coppery with lamplight. The air was warm, swarming with insects. Bats knifed through the darkness, scooping up mosquitoes, mashing them with tiny bloodied teeth in a silent airborne killing spree.

A dog yapped somewhere down the street. A couple passed, arm in arm, on the opposite side, their whispered talk barely audible.

Raider already had misgivings about this case, and now that he knew he might be facing a bunch of Kansas jay-hawkers, he had even less taste for it. Of course, there was no proof that Mantooth was out of Kansas, but those years after the war had seen a lot of thieves and plunderers taking advantage of the confusion of Reconstruction. Missouri had paid a high price for its allegiance to the Confederacy, and Arkansas as well had many wounds to lick.

The boardinghouse was well lighted at that hour, and the sign hanging from the roof eaves told Raider he'd reached his destination. Two young ladies sat in the porch swing, chatting, while two or three others sat on cane chairs behind the railing.

"Evenin' ladies," he said, tipping his shoddy hat. "Mrs. Skaggs about?"

"Yes, sir, she's in the parlor," said one of the girls on the swing.

Raider looked them over. They all wore the simple dresses of the working girl and seemed to be in their late teens or early twenties. He walked up the wide steps and knocked on the front door.

"Just go right on in," said a blond girl in a cane chair. "There's a bell on the hall table you can jangle."

Raider opened the door. There was a coat tree, a parasol stand and a small table that, indeed, had a small brass bell atop its polished surface. He picked it up and rattled the clapper. He heard sounds of muffled giggling on the front porch.

A tall woman appeared at the end of the short hallway. Hanging beads rattled from her passing through them to the foyer.

She was comely—beautiful, even—with ringlets of dark hair dangling in front of her ears, large brown eyes, a full bosom. She wore a flouncy skirt and a tight-fitting blouse that hugged her breasts.

"Mrs. Skaggs?"

"I'm Elinore Skaggs. State your business, sir."

"Uh, well, it's private and personal, ma'am."

She looked him up and down scathingly.

"Who sent you?"

"Uh, that's private and personal too." He took off his hat and tried his best to look humble.

"Very well," she said. "I'll give you five minutes." Her speech was refined, her diction impeccable. Raider followed her through the beaded curtain into the small parlor. Elinore Skaggs sat at a small desk where she had obviously been going over her accounts.

She waved him to an upholstered, straight-backed chair. A fancy lamp threw a glowing light over the room, holding the shadows at bay.

"Now," she said, "why are you here? This is a boardinghouse for young ladies, and we have strict rules."

"I'm inquiring about one of your former boarders, Molly Clemson."

"Yes?"

"Did you know her? Her family?"

"I'm sorry. We don't give out information about our girls. Besides, you haven't told me your name nor your business."

"My name is Raider. I'm a private investigator."

Elinore's eyebrows lifted in disbelief.

"Indeed, sir? What firm?"

"The Pinkerton National Detective Agency."

A look came over her face. A fleeting shadow.

"I—I, uh, I'm surprised. You look, well, ah, rather like a . . . a . . ."

"I know, a tramp. Look, ma'am, I can bring Sheriff Wales in here and force you to tell me what I need to know. I'm just trying to make it easy on both of us."

Mrs. Skaggs let out a sigh. Again she scrutinized Raider closely, as if trying to make up her mind whether to believe him or not.

"What do you want to know?" she said finally.

"Anything you can tell me."

He leaned forward, twirling his hat between his fingers. Elinore looked down at her desk, then back at him.

"She just came here. Moved in. We—we have a lot of girls who like to stay here."

"You don't say much."

"Molly, she's—she was a nice girl. A—a hard worker. I really can't say much about her. She's not bad. I don't see why you have to ask so many questions."

Raider felt sure that Mrs. Skaggs was holding something back. But he didn't know why. He decided to take another tack.

"Did Molly pick up her things when she left?"

"Yes." Very tight-lipped.

Raider moved in, shooting in the dark.

"Do you think Molly went back to Arkansas?"

Mrs. Skaggs fell into it. The question didn't seem a surprise to her.

"Oh, I know she did. She left a forwarding address."

Elinore handed Raider a scrap of paper.

The scrawled handwriting said simply: Molly Clemson, % Paul Stone, Harrison, Arkansas.

"Did she ever have any male visitors?"

"Mr. Raider . . . come now."

"Well, did she?"

"I—I can't recall. I don't think so."

Something was wrong. Raider could sense that Mrs. Skaggs was being less than truthful. However, he knew he would get no further with her. He got up from his chair.

"If you think of anything, I'll be at the Magnolia Hotel for a few days."

"What was Molly supposed to have done?" There was a wariness in her voice. There was also a trace of familiarity. Raider would have bet hard cash that Molly hadn't been just another boarder.

Raider looked at her sharply.

"I think she may have been involved in at least four killings, Mrs. Skaggs."

He was not preparped for Elinore's reaction. She had been fairly composed, despite a certain discomfiture. Now, however, her face drained to chalk, and she brought both hands up to her mouth as if to stifle a cry.

"Are—are you sure?"

"No, ma'am. I'm not sure of anything, except I think you're holding out on me. And I'm going to think about that for a while and wonder."

He waited a moment, sure that she was going to say something. Her mouth moved, but no sound came out.

"Good evening, Mrs. Skaggs," he said politely. "And thank you for your help."

"I—I'll see you to the door."

"I can find it," he said, stalking from the room. He rattled the beads extra loudly as he left. His boots boomed hollow on the hardwood floor. He slammed the front door and didn't bother tipping his hat to the women on the porch. All the way back to the hotel he kept thinking of Elinore Skaggs and Molly Clemson. At first appearance, there seemed to be no connection between the two, beyond tenant and land-lady. But he had seen something else in Mrs. Skaggs' eyes, just for a moment, a brief moment.

He knew what it was.

Fear.

The message, delivered over the Western Union wires to Doc Weatherbee, was succinct:

> DOSSIERS ON BEALE AND MANTOOTH SENT SPECIAL
> MESSENGER STOP ARRIVING TOMORROW VIA FRISCO
> RAIL STOP IMPORTANT RAIDER GO UNDERCOVER STOP
> HASTE URGENT STOP WAGNER.

Doc read the message again. His scalp crawled. Wagner might as well have shouted out that they were in a dangerous situation. Special messenger, indeed. And telling them to hurry. That meant that Allan Pinkerton himself was breath-ing down their necks. And they wanted to put Raider in with the gang. It was fairly unusual to be ordered to go undercover, and that's why Doc had checked back. He didn't want to make any mistakes, and since the bombing, he hadn't wanted to put his partner in jeopardy.

But now the die was cast. Raider would have to go down into the Ozarks and try and get in with a brutal gang of renegades.

Doc shuddered. It was not an easy thing to ask a friend

to do. One false move and Raider would be dead. And maybe himself as well.

He lit a cheroot as he walked away from the telegraph office, then set the match to the telegram.

He couldn't wait to see what was in those dossiers.

Raider knocked on Doc's door for fifteen minutes, then gave it up.

"To hell with it," he said.

He was weary. It had been a long day. He went to his own room, lit the lamp, and kicked off his boots. There was a table in the room, and two chairs. He threw his hat on the table and rubbed his forehead where the sweatband had left a mark. So far he had learned nothing to help the case. And he didn't know what his next move would be. That would depend on Wagner. If they wanted him to go down to Arkansas, he'd go, but he'd have to plan well. He couldn't just walk up to Mantooth and say he was an outlaw. Somehow he'd have to cultivate someone local who was familiar with the bunch. Someone who would recommend him. Someone who would lie in his teeth.

Raider peeled off his shirt and checked himself in the mirror. The beard was coming in, thickening on his cheeks and chin. He ran strong fingers through the hair on his chest. He looked, he thought, just straggly enough to pass for an Ozarker. Another week and he'd look like he'd never left the hills.

The shoes came off next. The socks. He left his pants on, in case Weatherbee showed up.

He was lying on the bed when the knock came.

Thinking it was Doc, he bounded to the door. But his instinct told him it wasn't Doc. The knock was too soft. There was no telltale smell of burning tobacco.

He waited.

The knock came again.

Raider stepped to one side of the door.

"Who is it?"

"Elinore Skaggs."

Something crackled in his brain.

He opened the door slightly and peered out.

"You alone?"

"Of course. Please, I must come in."

Raider let her in. He didn't lock the door. Elinore had changed clothes and was now garbed in a drab skirt and blouse. She wore a veil over her face. She clutched a purse in her hands.

"What's wrong? You think of something you didn't tell me?"

She pulled the veil over the top of her cloche. She took off the hat and shook out her hair.

"I—I couldn't speak freely before, Mr. Raider," she said. "When you told me that Molly might be involved in murder, I just—just choked up."

"Why? What does she mean to you?"

"May I sit down I—I feel weak. And—a little scared."

Raider pulled a chair away from the lone table in the room. She sat down. Raider took the other chair, suddenly very interested in what Elinore Skaggs had to say.

"Go on," he urged.

"Molly—she's my brother's daughter. Although she's my niece, she—she's like a sister to me. She married a man named Norville Clemson, against my brother's wishes. He's a widower, so I practically raised Molly. But I hadn't seen her since she ran off and married Clemson."

"Who is he?"

"A no account. My maiden name is Reynolds. My husband was killed in a mining accident at Lead Hill. We're— my family—is from Jasper, Arkansas. Tim Reynolds is my brother. He owns a mercantile store in Jasper."

"I know the place. So what did Molly tell you when she came to stay with you?"

Elinore couldn't take her eyes off Raider's bare chest. Her eyes refocused as she met his gaze.

"Nothing, actually. I gathered she was in financial trouble, needed a job. I tried to ask her about Norville, wondering if she had left him, but she said they were still married. When I asked her what he did for a living, she was vague."

"What exactly did she say?"

Elinore threw her head back and took a deep breath.

"She said he was in the hauling business."

"Freight?"

"I—I guess so. Mr. Raider, I know Molly. She's a good girl. How could she have—"

"—murdered someone? She didn't do the actual killing herself, if that's what you mean. But she's involved with a dangerous outfit. I don't know what Clemson is hauling, but it's probably stolen goods."

"What are you going to do?"

"I'm going to break up the gang. Arrest those I can."

"How?"

"That depends a lot on you, Mrs. Skaggs."

She looked at him with wet eyes.

"What about Molly?"

"I'll try to see that she gets fair treatment."

She paused and let out a breath.

"I—I'll do anything you ask, then."

Slowly she removed her hat and laid it on the table next to Raider's battered hat. When she stood up she put a hand on a button of her blouse. She began working the button free of the hole.

Her hand was trembling.

CHAPTER SIX

Elinore's breasts rose and fell with her heavy breathing.

Her trembling fingers worked the buttons on her blouse free, until her breasts tumbled into view. Raider gazed at the creamy, melon-round breasts, the areolae dark, the nipples jutting tautly. He stood up and stepped around the table.

"Mister..."

"It's just Raider," he husked.

"Raider...I can't help myself. You don't know what you do to a lonely woman."

He slid her blouse from her shoulders. Her flesh trembled when he touched her. He worked the loop loose in the back of her skirt, heard it whisper to the floor. Her hands flew to his trousers, began unbuckling his belt.

She stepped out of her shoes.

Raider tugged on her petticoat. She wore no panties.

His pants fell to the floor.

"How long has it been?" he asked.

"A year. Longer. Too long."

"Yes," he breathed, taking her into his arms. He kissed her. Her breasts deflated against his chest.

"Take me, take me," she whispered.

Elinore clutched his naked body desperately, crushing him to her breasts, kissing him hungrily, with an almost savage fervor. Raider's loins swarmed with heat. His cock grew bone hard, nudged the thatch between her legs. He drew her to him, caught up in her rabid passion. Her dark hair fell over her bare shoulders like a shawl. Her hands plucked at him frantically.

"You're about as ready as a woman can get," he rasped.

"Yes, yes," she breathed. "Take me now."

"The bed's right over there," said Raider.

Elinore was too much woman to carry, too tall. Besides, if he lifted her up in his arms, he wasn't sure they could make it that far. He wanted her so bad he was about to jump her where she stood.

"Yes," she said dreamily. She turned away and walked toward the bed like a somnambulist. He followed her, fascinated by the view of her buttocks. They were flawless, high-riding global hemispheres attached to long, lean legs. Whatever else Elinore was, she was a champion. Every line of her was thoroughbred woman.

Mrs. Skaggs flung herself on the bed and rolled until she was on her back. Her breasts were full and rounded, the nipples pertly taut. When she drew breath, her tummy flattened. He looked at her form, at the dark thatch between her legs, the mound underneath, pooching out invitingly. Blood throbbed in the blue veins of his swollen cock.

She opened her arms in a gesture of beckoning.

"You're some woman," he said, a terrible catch in his throat. Her flesh was tawny gold in the lamplight, her hair dark as a crow's wing, spread over the pillow like a fan. "There doesn't seem to be any end to you."

"If you're going to go after those men in Arkansas," she said, "you'll have to get back your accent."

"There don't seem to be no end to you," he drawled, a smile flickering on his lips.

She was pretty smart, after all, he decided.

Elinore smiled.

He crawled into bed with her. It was like stepping into a wildcat's den.

Her opened arms closed around his shoulders and back. She drew him atop her, thrusting upward with her hips. Their loins made contact, meshing in an urgent crush of flesh. She moved her hips, undulated her pussy, rubbed the fine wiry hairs against his swollen cock. Her mouth attached itself to his like a suction cup.

"I love the feel of your pecker against me," she crooned. "Oh, Raider, it's been so long."

A trace of bitterness, of sad longing, in her words.

"This pecker fits most anyplace," he said with a trace of sarcasm.

"I know. I want it inside me. Deep inside."

"You don't talk Arkansas much yourself"

"I was the one in the family they sent to school. Umm, I like your mouth, too. Your kiss." Her hands kneaded the back of his neck. "And you're strong. Like a bull. Like a stallion. My first impression of you wasn't favorable, you know. But behind that scraggly beard, you're one big hunk of man."

"Yes'm," he teased.

Elinore talked more like a schoolmarm than a landlady, but he supposed there was a similarity in the professions.

"Oh, Raider, you're funning me."

He wanted her. He wanted to plunge his cock between her legs, bury it in her soft flesh. The last thing he wanted to do was take her mind off what they both wanted. He gathered, however, that the lady was not quite ready.

"A minute ago," he said, "you wanted me bad. I feel the same. I'm ready. Anytime you are."

"Yes, yes, I know. But a woman needs to be held, to be touched, to feel wanted, to—"

He gripped her to him, encircling her back with his hands. He bore down on her mouth, and her kiss was full of steam and scent. She writhed in his embrace, her hips working, her loins pressing against his, her pussy thrusting upward, rubbing up and down the smooth length of his stiffened manhood.

It was too much for her.

She opened to him, spreading her legs wide.

"Now, now," she begged. "Hurry..."

Raider rose above her, dragged himself into position, his prick poised above her sex-cleft.

He drove into her smoothly, parting the soft labials, sinking into the fleshy pudding of her cunt. Her legs rose up in the air. She jolted with a sudden, shattering spasm.

Elinore's first orgasm crackled through her body like chain lightning. She bucked and thrashed in the clutch of an ecstatic seizure, her fingers raking narrow crimson streaks down Raider's back.

He pinned her shoulders to the bed and rode out the tidal-force quakes, plunging deep inside her each time she thrust her hips upward. She made strange animal-like sounds in her throat. Her eyes rolled in their sockets. Her face and neck crimsoned under the flushing heat of her passion. She squeezed him with the muscles in her legs, her pussy alive with sporadic contractions.

"You do grip a man, woman," he said.

Elinore, lost in the throes of delirium, did not reply.

She was a woman too long deprived of a man's affec-tions. He had seen the essence of her need in dozens of women. He had seen quiet, reserved, usually shy women turned into wild wantons after months or years of physical and sexual deprivation. But he had seldom seen one like Elinore Skaggs, who seemed oblivious to everything but the driving thrust of his cock. She seemed determined to skewer herself on his rod and twist mindlessly like spitted game roasting over an open fire. Her eyes flashed, and her body scraped against his like velvet flint against iron.

He sank into deep blazing seas and felt blood tingle through the stud-bone that sprouted from his loins, felt that same blood pound in his temples like a hammering ocean tide, boom in his heart like some pagan drum.

Elinore was insatiable, merciless in her pursuit of gratification. Her body drove like a quarter horse toward an unseen finish line, like a canoe caught in wild rapids, shooting downstream at full race.

He lost track of her shattering climaxes. Swept up in the savagery of her lust, he stayed his own climax with a sheer effort of will.

The two rocked together as one, while she pleaded with her body for his seed. He felt it coming, knew she wanted him to explode inside her like the sudden eruption of a volcanic mountain, like a cyclonic rush of twisting air over Kansas in March.

She cried out for him and screamed in his ear, her voice drowning out the awesome throb-roar of blood in his tympanum.

"Raider, yes, yes, now, now!" she shrieked. "Give it to me. Give it all to me!"

He could no longer hold back. He gave up his will. His boiling, shooting seed and a thousand winds shattered his eardrums with sound as if his blood had burst open his veins, as if he was a man struck by a cannonball, splitting open and dying at the very moment when life was sweetest.

He swore softly, mashed fingertips into the small of her back, and drew her quivering hips into his. He gave up his seed in a volcanic spew, and it was like giving up some part of his life, some piece of his soul. It was violent and wonderful and made him feel good because he was in her arms and she was close against him, stuck to him like flypaper, holding on to him with desperate loving arms.

Raider shuddered in the throes of pleasure.

Elinore gasped and bucked one last time. She fell away from him then, lifeless as a rag doll.

He swore again, under his breath.

"Woman," he gasped, and the word was full of praise and gratitude.

She gave him a last squeeze, released him.

"You're sweet as a spring persimmon," she drawled, reverting to her native accent. "You pleasured me right well, and I'm fully beholden to you."

He looked into her blue eyes with wonder.

"Child," he soothed, "you're plumb honeycomb."

They laughed together, like children after play.

"Ah, you're Arkansas again," she said. "You make me feel homesick."

He rolled off her and lay on his back beside her.

"Maybe I've been away too long at that," he said. "Could be I ought to go home again sometime soon."

She let out a sighing breath.

"You almost make me want to go back," she replied, a trace of sadness in her voice, the accent there, strong as a young oak shoot sprouting from a cut stump.

They lay there, basking in the backwash of their love tussle. Their hands roamed sweat-sodden flesh, secret places, dark crevices.

Raider wanted her again.

Elinore turned to him, threw a leg over his crotch.

He bent to her breasts, took a nipple between his lips. He nibbled on it, felt it turn hard as a chinquapin.

The door opened silently.

The man in the pewter-gray cassimere suit, wearing a curled-brim derby, peeked in, his eyes glittery bright with mischief.

"Oh lordy, Raider," he mocked with a simulated southern accent. "If Allan Pinkerton could only see you now. In your natural state."

Raider looked up, startled.

Elinore tried to shrink into the bedclothes, hide behind Raider's naked bulk.

"You bastard," Raider said evenly. "You no-good Yankee sonofabitch."

Weatherbee smiled crookedly.

"Now, now," he said. "Don't get testy. Your door was open."

"You didn't knock."

"Ever so lightly. In case, ah, you were asleep."

"My ass," said Raider.

"Indeed."

Again, Doc flashed the same crooked smile.

An evil smile, thought Raider.

A lewd smile, thought Elinore.

This time, Doc was in his room when Raider knocked.

He opened the door.

Raider threw the punch from shoulder height. His fist caught Doc square in the chin.

Weatherbee shot backwards six feet and crashed into the table in the center of the room. He fell in a clatter of glasses, a brandy bottle, a humidor full of cheroots, and his notebook.

Raider stalked into the room, tucking in his shirt-tail.

Doc rubbed his jaw.

"What the hell was that for?" he asked groggily.

"That's for not knocking. I'm saving up another one."

"For what?"

"For the next time you bust in on me when I'm putting the boots to a lady."

Doc groaned and pulled himself to his feet.

"You're always *in flagrante delicto,* my friend, so you better take your punch now."

Raider hauled back, ready to accommodate Doc.

Weatherbee held up both hands and ducked his head.

"Just joshing, my boy, just joshing."

"Well, watch yourself, Doc. I'm in a mean mood. That woman was good for the rest of the night."

"Ah, but not you, Raider. You're leaving for Arkansas. Tonight."

"Tonight? What's the rush?"

Doc told him about the telegram from Wagner.

"So?" said Raider. "I can just get on down there in the morning. Leave at a more decent hour. It'd be midnight before I could leave."

"No, I've got a horse hitched out front for you. A poor horse, to be sure, because you have to look the part, my boy."

"The horse probably could use some sleep too. I don't see what in hell the all-fired rush is about."

"It's about Duane Beale," said Doc soberly. "There's no need to wait for that dossier on him."

"Huh?"

"An hour ago, Sheriff Edwin Wales and his two deputies, Smith and Meadows, rode over to his place to put him in custody until that special messenger arrives tomorrow on the Frisco train. I thought it might save us some trouble."

"All right. So you got Beale in the *juzgado.*"

"Ah, but that's the hitch. Beale didn't take kindly to the intrusion. He shot it out with Edwin and his cohorts. Hal Meadows has a lead ball in his lower back. Bob Smith has an arm half shot off, and Wales is leaking from both legs."

"Christ. What about Beale?"

Doc fished a gold watch from his vest pocket.

"He's got about a half hour on you, I figure. But you can catch him if you hurry. There's a tavern in Hollister where you and I will make contact when necessary. It's called the Red Lion."

"Is that where Beale is headed?"

Doc smiled enigmatically and shook his head.

"I doubt it. He's probably riding hell bent for leather straight for the Arkansas border. And you'd better get on that horse down there and catch him before he gets there."

"Why? Can't they get a posse up? I mean, the man shot up three lawmen. They must want him pretty bad."

Weatherbee sighed.

"Don't you get it, Raider? Beale knows me. He's going down there to tell Mantooth just who I am. I have to have some room to move around too. If you're going to work undercover, you'll need to make contact."

A look came over Raider's face.

He didn't say anything.

Before Doc knew it, he was gone.

CHAPTER SEVEN

It took Raider ten minutes to get his gear together.

While he was packing, Doc gave him a full description of Beale. From Wales, Doc had learned that the man rode a big Missouri bay.

As he mounted up, a figure separated from the shadows and came out to see him.

It was Elinore.

"Are—are you going?"

"Yes." He couldn't see her face. It was hidden behind a veil. "South."

"I figured you would. Raider, I wish you well. I know you're going to need help. Here, take this."

She handed him a folded-up piece of paper. He couldn't read it in the dark.

"When you get down there," she said, "look up the person named in my note. She can help."

"She?"

Elinore said no more. She scurried away, back into the

57

shadows, before he could find out what she meant.

The horse Doc had left hitched at the rail wasn't much, but it had good legs and a sound chest. Raider had his rifle, pistol, and bedroll stowed away. Now he hoped he could find the fastest trail south to the Arkansas border. By now, he figured, Beale had at least an hour's head start on him, maybe more.

The main road out of Springfield was the Harrison-Springfield road. It was the quickest route, and that's the one Raider took in his pursuit of Duane Beale. There were alternate roads, but Raider's hunch was that Beale would take the main freight route through Reno. What he wondered now was whether or not Beale would stop over in Spokane. It was a long ride to Harrison: ten days for a freighter, hard going at night. He figured the man would at least pass through the highlands and Ozark, especially if he figured he had a posse on his trail. A posse, he knew, would be hard to round up at this hour of the night. Likely, Beale would figure no one would come after him until daybreak.

The odds were already against Raider, but his mind was working rapidly as the sorrel gelding Doc had given him chewed up the miles in a loping gait.

Raider checked off the towns he would go through in his mind. If Beale stuck to the main freight road, he would make better time. But Beale wasn't made of iron. He'd have to stop somewhere. And, for damned sure, he'd be looking at his backtrail. The man might even be lying in wait now, ready to shoot the first rider coming south in a hurry.

This last thought gave Raider pause. Maybe, thought the Pinkerton, he was going at this all wrong. Maybe the way to get Beale was to stop chasing him.

After all, Beale didn't know Raider. He only knew Doc. So far as he knew, he had never laid eyes on the man. But, though Raider himself might still work undercover even if

Beale tipped off Mantooth about Weatherbee, Doc's life wouldn't be worth a plugged nickel once he crossed the border into Arkansas.

And that man Peters hadn't even gotten over the border. He had been thought a Pinkerton, though he wasn't, and now he was dead.

Doc looked through the mass of papers retrieved from Beale's office.

One thing was certain—Beale had wanted to cover his tracks. He fully expected to get by with the robbery of that three thousand dollars. Hence, he had hired three hardcases to guard the freight wagon. After, of course, it had crossed the White River. This wasn't hard evidence, Doc knew, but the move was so unusual that it bore coming under hard scrutiny.

He walked through the rubble of Beale's outer office, trying to puzzle it together. After an almost sleepless night, he had gotten up early to try and sift through Beale's files. He wondered too what Paul Stone's connection was. Was he in this with Beale? Or had he just been gulled? He could find no proof of collusion. Yet Stone's freighters had been ignored by the redlegs. Until the theft of the $3,000.

And where was Stone now?

In Harrison, presumably.

Doc took photographs of the blast-shattered offices with his Premo Sr. camera. Wagner might find them interesting. They could later be used for evidence, if necessary.

Back at the hotel, Doc waited for the special messenger. He wondered whether Raider had caught up to Beale or walked into an ambush. He had smoked a cheroot down to a butt before the messenger arrived.

"You Weatherbee?"

"Yes." Doc stood at the door of his room at the Magnolia

Hotel. But his Studebaker was packed and ready to go south.

"These are for you, then. Sign here."

Doc scrawled his name on the man's receipt and took the bulky packet from him.

"I got a personal message for you too," said the courier, a faceless man in his thirties.

"What's that?"

"Your expense draft is in the post."

Doc laughed drily.

"I know. The check's in the mail. Thanks."

Doc closed the door, sat down at the table, and broke open the packet.

He read the dossier on Mantooth first.

The report made Weatherbee's skin crawl. Mantooth had first come to the government's attention prior to the Civil War. While still a young man, he had been involved in the Kansas-Missouri border wars of the 1850s. When the war broke out, Seth joined the United States Army. Like many others of his ilk, he pledged allegiance to the United States, wore a Union uniform, drew Union soldier's pay, only to take up arms against the people of western Missouri and northwest Arkansas in a wanton spree of personal vengeance.

The jayhawkers, led by despicable Kansas officers, roamed freely over the countryside, "stealing every horse, slave, or movable object that suited their fancy."

Doc was surprised at the strange quirk of events that pitted Kansas jayhawkers against William Clarke Quantrill's Confederate guerrillas. Quantrill, who often had his men wear Union uniforms as a disguise, was every bit as evil as the jayhawkers he clashed with, indulging in murder, rape, and robbery, as well as arson.

A report from General Henry W. Halleck, who took over command of the Union forces in Missouri, with headquarters in St. Louis, summed up the situation. In his General Order #13, he charged that:

"The Rebels in the Southwestern counties of this state have robbed and plundered the peaceful noncombatants, taking from them their clothing and means of subsistence. Men, women, and children have alike been stripped and plundered. Thousands of such persons are finding their way to this city barefooted, half clad, and in a destitute and starving condition."

The depredations continued, and Mantooth was in the thick of it, taking part in raids down in Arkansas as far south as Fayetteville.

The jayhawkers sealed their unsavory reputation, however, with the infamous raid on Osceola, Missouri, a small town of two or three thousand souls near the Kansas border.

Doc knew some of the background. James H. Lane, the U.S. senator from Kansas, was a fanatical abolitionist. He prevailed upon President Lincoln at the beginning of the war to grant him permission to raise an army of volunteers from among his constituents.

Lane quickly formed an army of thugs, promising an abundance of booty and unrestricted vengeance against the hated Missourians. With his ragtag "army" of cutthroats, Lane marched from Ft. Scott, Kansas, toward the Missouri border. When he and his men crossed the border, Lane gave them their orders: "Everything disloyal, from a Shanghai rooster to a Durham cow, must be cleaned out."

On September 22, 1861, Lane's troopers descended on Osceola. Among the men were some that Wagner had encircled on the documents—Duane Beale, Hobart Stamper, Lazarus Benteen, Norville Clemson, and Paul Stone. Doc's eyebrows lifted as he continued reading the account.

First the town was searched thoroughly and systematically. Mantooth and Stone located gunpowder and lead.

They were treated like heroes by the Kansas volunteers, and a hue and cry arose that gave Lane a pretext for setting up the chain of events that followed.

A drumhead court was quickly established, and nine citizens were brought up for court martial. These were tried, found guilty, and shot. Lane ordered all available wagons, buggies, carts—anything with wheels—confiscated and used to clean out the town's stores. Homes were pillaged as well. Among the choice items were several barrels of brandy.

When all the valuables had been loaded onto conveyances, the town was fired. The courthouse, with all of the county records, was destroyed. Over one million dollars worth of property was either appropriated or burned to the ground. Only three houses were spared, seemingly owned by Union sympathizers. However, Union and Confederate sympathizers alike were treated roughly by the Kansans while wearing Union uniforms and flying the flag of the United States of America.

Wagner had scrawled something in the margin.

"When the Kansans left Osceola," he wrote, "their train contained, besides household goods and merchandise stolen from the stores, 400 head of cattle, 350 horses, 200 Negroes. A fine carriage was delivered to Lane's family in Lawrence. The wagons were also crammed with about 300 'soldiers' too drunk to march."

So there it was, thought Doc. All of them together. Names he knew only from hearsay, a new one or two. Perhaps a relative of Molly Clemson's. Men who had marched into Osceola with Jim Lane. The name Hobart Stamper was familiar. Dover had mentioned him. There was only one name missing, one that he had expected would be there.

Seth Mantooth was not on the list.

But there was more.

The men rode with Charles Jennison's jayhawkers, who, under the command of Major Daniel R. Anthony, started "committing depredations upon Unionists and secessionists indiscriminately. They have burned 42 houses in that vicinity [of Central Missouri] and robbed others of valuables and driven off livestock. . . . To cap the climax, they shot to death Mr. Richards, a good Union man, without cause or provocation."

The men know the country. Doc read a communiqué from Colonel John S. Phelps to General Halleck, outlining the various problems with rebels, but Wagner seemed to think that jayhawkers were posing as rebels when it suited them.

Halleck seemed to agree. In a letter to Secretary of War E. M. Stanton, he expressed his displeasure and intentions: "The Kansas jayhawkers, or robbers, who were organized under the auspices of Senator James H. Lane wear the uniform of and it is believed receive pay from the United States. Their principal occupation for the last six months seems to have been the stealing of Negroes, the robbing of homes, and burning of barns, grain, and forage. The evidence of their crimes is unquestionable. They have not heretofore been under my orders. I will now keep them out of Missouri or have them shot."

Doc raced through the dossier now, curious about Seth Mantooth, who had not been mentioned in the account thus far. Yet Wagner had selected a half-dozen names as important and made notations about them in the margins. Beale and Stone, in particular, seemed to have known each other long before they had taken a building in Springfield to promote their businesses.

What was going on here? What was behind the seemingly disconnected events down along the Arkansas border? What connection was there between a freight company based in

Harrison, with an office in Springfield, and a guard company that now seemed to be as crooked as a country creek?

Doc turned a page, and there it was.

Not all of it yet, but the beginnings.

Seth Mantooth.

He came from Jasper, Arkansas, Doc read, but he was a rebel from boyhood. Like Beale, Clemson, Stamper, Benteen, and Stone, he fought on the Union side at first. Then they switched their allegiance to the Confederacy. And Mantooth was behind it all. He was their leader, their persuader. Mantooth formed these men into a lawless, savage, reckless fighting group and took them to ride with an even more ruthless man, William Clarke Quantrill.

Doc read on, his heart pumping, his stomach swirling with moths.

This was what he needed to know.

This was information that might keep Raider from getting killed. Now, Weatherbee wondered if he had done right in sending his partner out after Beale. It was a long shot at best.

But of course Beale had to be stopped. If he got through to Mantooth, Raider might never infiltrate the gang. Two men were needed to stop these killers. One on the inside: Raider. The other on the outside: Weatherbee.

It was that simple.

And it was dangerous.

CHAPTER EIGHT

Duane Beale was canny.

He holed up in a place called Walnust Shade just in case someone was trailing him. There he could see any rider coming down from either Reno or Spokane. He doubted that any pursuers would be so foolish as to take the Boston road. It was the longest route from Springfield for anyone going to Harrison.

He had ridden hard and fast. Now his horse was lathered and breathing heavily. But no rider had come up on him in the night, and he had slept half a day before going on. Last night he had ridden straight through, in the cool. Now, in the heat of morning, his horse needed rest and so did he.

Beale chewed on a chunk of jerky as he walked his horse through the waters of Bull Creek under the shade of trees. His stomach was still in knots, his hunger a raw gnashing in his gut. He didn't make a smoke, and he carried a rifle in one hand. All the time he kept looking up the road. A caravan of freighters passed without noticing him.

Flies droned in the bushes. Beale brushed off a wood tick that had attacked itself to his trouser leg. The horse switched its tail, batting at insects.

The sun climbed in the sky.

A family going the other way, toward Spokane, passed slowly in a rattley Springfield wagon loaded with chickens. He heard the fowls squawking for a long time after the family passed.

The horse cooled down. Beale finished chewing on the jerky and drank from the stream. He let the horse graze on a short rope. He wanted to be able to mount up and move fast. He tied one end of the tether to a sapling and leaned against a tree.

He waited, his eyes on the bridge that spanned Bull Creek. He could stand off a posse from his position for a long time, if need be. Anyone coming across the bridge would be in the open, unable to hide.

Beale shifted the rifle in his hands.

His palms began to sweat.

Raider knew something was wrong.

The minute his horse's hooves hit the bridge, the hackles on the back of his neck began to rise. The hooves made a hollow wooden sound on the dried boards.

Some instinct in him told Raider to slow down, to think. Above all, *don't look around*. He narrowed his eyes, moved slowly across the small bridge. When he reached the other side, he cut back and rode down to the creek's edge.

It was quiet.

Raider drew a deep breath and looked around casually as if he had all the time in the world, as if he didn't have a care.

He didn't scan the creek bottom too intently.

Yet something crawled on the back of his neck.

He knew damned well someone was watching him.

Then he saw the slight movement. The falling sun of late afternoon glinted on something shiny off in the trees, beyond the arbor of dripping leaves that drooped over the gurgling creek.

He was glad now he hadn't pushed it. The man in the trees stood half hidden in the cottonwoods on the opposite bank. Had Raider been riding fast over the bridge, the watcher would have had a clear, easy shot.

Right in the back.

Raider's blood turned cold, but he made no sign that he saw the man in the trees. He was almost dead certain now that the sun's rays were striking a rifle barrel, glancing off with a blinding flash. Out of the corner of his eye he saw what looked to be a horse grazing back in the shadows.

Something told Raider that if he made one false or suspicious move the man in the trees would shoot him dead.

He patted the horse's withers and squatted slowly to scoop up a double handful of water from the brook. He drank and splashed his face. He moved at a deliberately leisurely pace; he avoided looking at the place where the man with the rifle was standing.

"Come on, boy," he said to the sorrel, knowing his voice, with its newly reacquired Arkansas accent, would carry across the branch. He climbed back up on the saddle and clucked to the gelding. Back on the road, he looked straight ahead, although he could feel the watcher's eyes burning into the back of his neck. He did not show any signs of hurry.

If that was Beale back there, he figured, the man would either catch up to him or wait some time longer in case a posse showed.

Raider, too, had ridden by night, grabbing catnaps in the saddle. His eyes were sore and red-rimmed from lack of sleep. But now his senses were fully alert, tuned up like a violin's strings, taut as stretched catgut.

If the man back there was Beale, he reasoned, then his own purpose had been accomplished. He was now between Beale and the Arkansas border. There was still the matter of detaining and arresting him, but so far so good. Except now, if that was indeed Beale, the hunted had become the hunter.

Raider made two miles before he heard the drumming beats of a horse's hooves. He turned and looked behind him. The rider was coming fast. Raider reined his horse over and moved to the side of the road as if to let the rider pass. Instead the oncoming horse slowed.

"Hold up there!" shouted the rider.

Raider brought the sorrel to a halt.

"Howdy," he said, in his friendliest tone. He couldn't bring himself to grin idiotically, but he did his best to put the man on the big bay horse at ease.

Raider got a good look at him as he rode up and reined his horse to a halt.

The man wasn't tall. His blue eyes bulged like plums from beneath thick lids that cowled them halfway. There were red streaks in the whites. A bulbous nose glistened with veiny rivers and lumpy blackheads. He sat like a keg on his saddle, licking lips that were thick and liverish. Sandy hair jutted from under his hat.

From Doc's description and his own observation, Raider was convinced that the man he faced was Duane Beale.

"Where you headed, stranger?" Beale's breath reeked of beef and whiskey.

"Hollister, I reckon."

"You from around there?" asked Beale.

"Nope. I'm from down Viola way."

"Where's that?" Raider was sure that Beale knew damned

well where it was. So, thank God, did he.

"On the south side of the White."

"Where's the ferry go down there?"

"Shell Knob," replied Raider, without a blink.

"You're a long ways from home, friend."

"I reckon so."

"Don't 'member seeing you around these parts."

"It's been a spell, all right."

Beale was parrying, thrusting. Raider volunteered no information. He knew the ways of the hill folks.

"Hollister, you say," said Beale, glancing over his shoulder, back toward the bridge. "I'm goin' that way myself. I'll ride with you." It wasn't a question; it sounded almost like an ultimatum.

Raider shrugged.

As the two men rode off, Raider had the feeling that he was Beale's prisoner.

The dossier on Seth Mantooth fairly dripped with blood.

Doc Weatherbee read it avidly, curious about the man the Pinkertons had sent him to hunt down and bring to justice.

His skin crawled as he read the copious notes from Wagner and various other investigators who had pieced together the background of a vicious killer.

Mantooth's name first surfaced when he rode with Quantrill, ostensibly for the Union forces. However, it was here that he met Stone, Benteen, Clemson, Beale, and Stamper. Apparently he persuaded these men to desert and return to the Confederacy, not as legitimate soldiers but as outlaws, bushwackers.

Mantooth, wrote one of the operatives, committed his first murder when he was twelve years old, living in Jasper, Arkansas. He shot a younger playmate to death, showing no remorse. Adults were afraid of him. After tasting blood, he seemed to want more. He killed at least eight people before he joined Quantrill's band. He feasted on war.

Doc noted those last words. He wondered now if he was hunting a robber and murderer or someone with bigger aspirations.

The account continued, surprisingly well documented.

Mantooth retreated back into Arkansas, joined up with an even more notorious killer, an infamous man named Alfred Bolin.

Alf Bolin, who was already an acknowledged outlaw at the outbreak of war, took up the Rebel cause with a peculiar, twisted vengeance. He and his gang fought Union soldiers, murdered the families of Unionists, and raped their women. Mantooth and his band joined Bolin and became assimilated into his gang of cutthroats. They operated in the mountainous country surrounding the bend in the White River.

Bolin and Mantooth robbed, raped, and murdered the people from Union families over a wide area between Ozark, Missouri, and Crooked Creek, Arkansas. A price was put on the heads of these men, which seemed to make them even bolder and more vicious.

When Bolin was killed, Mantooth took over the gang.

"He was never captured," wrote Wagner. "And many still fear him. We have evidence that he is in Jasper, Arkansas, but no one thus far has spoken of his hideout. Those who have come forward were killed before they could relate any solid information."

Doc sighed deeply.

Now he knew more about the man he and Raider were facing.

The remainder of the dossier contained information he had already determined from talking to Dover.

"Every attempt to pursue Mantooth, following a robbery, has ended at a dead end. The man is like smoke. He seems to be able to disappear into thin air."

Doc snorted.

The man wasn't superhuman. There had to be a reason for his disappearances.

Mantooth knew the country. The Ozarks were a wild place, full of hidden valleys, hollows, and steep, rugged hills. Somehow, Weatherbee reasoned, he was making full use of the terrain to make good his escapes. But there was more to it than that. Doc knew he was missing something. Something important.

He put away the papers and made his plans.

The next day he hitched Judith to the Studebaker and bought supplies for the journey south. He went to see Edwin Wales, who was recovering from the bullet holes in his legs.

Wales was laid up in his bed at home. His wife, Sandra, set Doc a chair by her husband's bedside.

"I'll need some information," said Doc.

"I'll give it gladly, if I can."

"I need to buy a dog."

"A dog?"

"Yes. A special kind of dog."

"What kind?"

"Bloodhound."

Beale's corpulence began to tell on him by late afternoon. Sweat rolled off him in rivulets. His clothes stuck to his skin.

And he was still suspicious of Raider.

"You never did tell me your name, stranger," he said as they made their way from Pedrow to the Boston ferry.

"Didn't get yours, neither," drawled the Pinkerton.

"Bascomb," lied Beale.

Raider gave no indication that the name meant anything to him one way or the other.

"They call me Nat Parker," said Raider without blinking an eye.

"The name Parker's common hereabouts."

"I reckon."

And that was all the information Beale got.

Raider knew he had to make his move soon. Before they reached the Arkansas border. As they crossed the White River on the Boston ferry, he made his plans. He had already told Beale that he was going to Hollister. But if Beale was going to Harrison, as Raider assumed he was, then he would continue on, leaving Raider to pursue him again. There had to be a way to apprehend Beale somewhere between the drop-off point of the ferry and the side road to Hollister.

"You said you were going on to Hollister," said Beale after they had crossed the river.

"I reckon so."

Beale wiped a gob of sweat off his forehead with his bandanna and squeezed it until it dripped.

"Maybe I'll lay up there a night."

"Suit yourself."

Beale kept looking over his shoulder, but the road was little traveled at that time of day. A freight wagon was broken down at the Kirbyville fork. Here Beale could either continue on or ride the short distance to Hollister along the ridge. The sun was already dropping toward the horizon.

Raider deliberately used no persuasion. By now Beale was as jumpy as a cat in a roomful of rocking chairs. And sweating profusely. Sweating until he stank to high heaven.

"You mind if I ride along, Parker?"

"Nope."

It was settled, then. Raider now knew that the tables had

turned once again. As far as he was concerned, Beale was his prisoner.

The two men rode into the sleepy little town, crossing the shallows of Turkey Creek. They came up behind the Red Lion. Across the street a row of buildings lined the road—a hotel, a boardinghouse, a blacksmith shop, a mercantile store.

"I'm going to wet my whistle," said Raider.

Beale licked dry lips.

For a moment the Pinkerton operative thought Beale wasn't going to accept the offhand invitation. If so, he might lose the opportunity to put the man in irons.

"Should put up the horses first. I could use a drink."

Raider breathed an inward sigh of relief.

The livery stable was at the end of the street. Both men walked back to the tavern. Raider towered over the shorter Beale.

"You say you're from Viola. Never heard of any Parkers down that way."

"Well, we're backwoods folks."

The tavern, made of native stone, was cool and dark. There were few people there, although a wagon and two mules were hitched out front. Two men sat at a table playing cards. Another man sat at the bar drinking beer,

The bartender looked up as Beale and Raider sat down.

"Howdy, Duane, ain't seed you in a spell."

"Afternoon, Charlie. Bring us a pail of beer and a couple of glasses. Beer cold?"

"It's wet," said Charlie.

"Beer okay with you, Parker."

Raider nodded.

It was time to make his move. Beale was off guard, among friends. There was only one problem.

Charlie.

CHAPTER NINE

Doc pulled into the road that led down to the small log farmhouse.

Following directions Sheriff Wales had given him, Doc had driven Judith down to Highlandville. In a sealed oilskin packet he carried warrants of arrest. The warrants had various real names on them. Some were blank.

These were concealed in a secret compartment under the wagon bed, where Doc had certain other items useful to a Pinkerton operative of his particular resourcefulness.

In the back of the wagon, above the secret flooring, Weatherbee had something else that was new: a wire and wood kennel, suitable for transporting a rather large dog. This he had picked up in Springfield, upon Sheriff Wales' recommendation. He also carried a wooden ammunition box full of bones he had gotten from a butcher, paying all of six bits for some thirty pounds of beef legs, joints, kneecaps, and tailbone.

The road twisted down the slope of a ridge. The farmhouse, made of logs that were bowed from weather, and chinked with small stones, wood shavings, and clay and mortar, teetered on a level piece of ground.

The noise was deafening as Doc pulled up beyond the rickety fence that encircled the yard. The fence was made of split rails stood upright in the ground, with whipsawed boards of varying sizes nailed up flat against the posts.

Dogs howled, barked, snarled, whined, growled, and wailed as Weatherbee set the hand brake.

"Hello, the house," he called.

He climbed down and went up to the gate, smoothing the lapels of his light tan coat and adjusting his silken ascot.

There was no answer.

He opened the creaking gate and walked through. The dogs in the kennels howled even more furiously than before.

"Anybody home?"

Doc looked up to the house and saw the ugly snout of a double-barreled shotgun slide through a window port.

He stopped in his tracks.

"Who are you and what do you want?" The voice was low, gravelly, and slightly muffled.

"Name's Doc Weatherbee. Came to see a Val Drews."

"We don't want no patent medicines. Take your wagon and get on out of here."

"Came to buy a dog."

"How's that?"

"I said I want to buy a bloodhound!" shouted Doc.

"Well, why didn't you say so?"

The shotgun slid back through the port of the shuttered window. Doc heard sounds from inside the house. A moment later the front door banged open. A woman, dressed in pants and a man's shirt, stepped onto the porch. Her fine auburn hair was drawn away from her face. She had hazel eyes, a pretty nose, even white teeth.

"Is Mr. Drews here?" asked Doc.

"There ain't no Mr. Drews. I'm Valerie Drews."

Doc muttered under his breath. Wales had told him only the name Val. Never mentioned that Val was a woman. A very pretty woman, at that.

"You the owner here?"

"I am. What's this about buying a bloodhound. What you want it for?" Her suspicious gaze wandered to his wagon with its gaudy lettering.

"Hunting," said Doc.

"These dogs only hunt one thing, mister. Human beings."

"Ah, can we talk? I fear I must be somewhat discreet."

The woman snorted. She appeared to be in her late twenties. Her face was scrubbed clean, and she wore no makeup.

"You talk pretty fancy. Not many city slickers come out this way. 'Specially ones wanting bloodhounds."

"Well, can we talk anyway?"

"Sure. Come on up. I've got a pot of coffee brewing."

Doc listened to the dogs and shuddered. They sounded as if they were going to break loose and kill everything in sight.

The front room of the cabin was neater than Doc expected. There was a divan, a chair, little pillows, a couple of small tables, a desk, and an oval rug in the center of the room. The furniture looked handmade, of wood and cloth sewn over stuffing of either fine wood shavings or feathers. A few pictures adorned the walls, drawings of hunting dogs, a Currier and Ives reproduction, some Audubon prints in rustic frames. Dried weeds and wildflowers sprouted from dusty vases.

"Come on back to the kitchen," said Val, disappearing through the opening to a narrow hallway.

Doc passed a couple of bedrooms and stumbled over a brass replica of a bloodhound. There were rough sketches of dogs hanging on the walls of the hallway.

The kitchen was spacious, encompassing a wide area that appeared to have once served as a dining room. Now an easel stood in the center, with a large window throwing light over the half-finished canvas. There was a small table next to the easel, crammed full of artist's materials—turpentine, linseed oil, brushes, pencils, paper pads, small jars of paint, charcoal sticks, oily rags, and palette.

"You're an artist, I see."

"I try," said Val. "Set yourself down."

The kitchen had a larger table, rough-hewn from pine. It was polished smooth. The chair was sturdy. Val banged a pot on the stove and rattled cups in the cupboards. There were kettles full of water already on the stove. Steam vapors floated above them.

"Nice place," said Doc.

"Not really. But I built it myself. It suits me."

"Yes." Doc looked at the painting half finished on the easel. It showed talent. The head of the bloodhound, with its droopy ears and big watery eyes, almost seemed to leap from the canvas, even in its unfinished state.

Val brought steaming cups of coffee to the table and took a chair across from Doc.

She saw him looking at her painting.

"That's Alf. Named after Alf Bolin."

"What do you do with your paintings?"

"Sell them, most of them. A man comes by here twice a year, takes what I have."

"You have talent."

"Thank you."

They sipped their coffee, sizing each other up across the table. Doc was impressed by this independent woman. She had built herself a home, was an accomplished artist, and raised hounds.

"Now, what was this about your wanting to buy a blood-hound?"

"I am prepared to purchase one, yes."

"Why?"

"I, ah, need it for a manhunt."

"One bloodhound?"

Doc looked sheepish.

"Anything wrong with that?" he asked.

"Sometimes one hound is enough. However, two are more reliable. Depends on who you're after. Generally, I don't sell my dogs except to other breeders. Too hard to train. But my services are for hire, if you're legitimate. You either have to be a lawman, or Army, or—"

"Would a Pinkerton do?"

Her eyebrows lifted.

"Who sent you here?"

Doc told her.

She let out a breath.

"I never met a dandy before. And now you say you're a Pinkerton to boot." She took a swallow of coffee and scratched her head. "Now I wonder who you're after."

Doc debated with himself about whether or not to tell Miss Drews the whole story. After all, she might be kin to those he sought. Still, without her bloodhounds he knew he had little chance of tracking down the elusive gang of cut-throats.

"I'm after a man named Mantooth," he said finally. "Seth Mantooth."

Val's expression changed. Her eyes widened; her complexion suffused with sudden crimson.

"Seth Mantooth? Are you plumb crazy, mister?"

"Why? Do you know the man?"

"Know him? No, not exactly. but there isn't anyone in

these here parts who doesn't know who he is. He—well, I'd better not talk out of school."

"No," said Doc, "please do. I'd be most grateful for any information you could give me."

Valerie regarded the Pinkerton for a long time before she spoke. Her eyes seemed to burn into his, to bore deep as if to determine whether or not she dared trust him.

"I don't know. It—it's not safe to say too much about that man."

Doc reached across the table and touched her hand. He knew that she had spoken truly. Dover had told him about Mantooth, and now he was dead. But he needed to know all he could. Right now, Valerie was his only lead. Even if she didn't know Mantooth personally she might have valuable information that would help in his capture. As a Pinkerton, he had learned to leave no stone unturned when investigating a case.

"Please," said Doc. "I'm afraid a lot of innocent people are going to die if this man isn't stopped."

"Yes, yes," she stammered, a faraway look dulling her eyes. She seemed to look beyond Weatherbee, fixing her gaze on some point in time, perhaps in the past. "If—if anyone knew I was telling you this . . ."

"Don't worry. A Pinkerton always honors confidentiality from witnesses."

"Huh?"

"We don't tell secrets."

Doc smiled at her and squeezed her hand encouragingly.

"All—right, all right," she said, letting out a long sigh. "But I really don't know very much. Just what I've heard, and . . . and . . . well, I'll tell you this: I don't think a bloodhound could track Seth Mantooth."

"Why not?"

"He—he knows these hills too well. He was born and reared in them, fought in them—on both sides, I heard tell. He knows what to lay down on his track to throw off the hounds. There was a man tried to get him with dogs about three years back. I—I knew the man. He had good hounds, raised blue ticks and redbones. But he had some bloods, too. In fact"—she paused, her eyes watering—"I have some of his . . ." She stopped, unable to continue.

Her eyes misted with sudden tears.

Doc quickly pulled a kerchief from an inside pocket of his coat and handed it to Val.

"Th-thank you," she said. "I'm sorry."

"Why was this man tracking Mantooth?" Doc persisted, his voice pitched low, the tone soothing.

"H—he said Mantooth sullied his sister."

"Sullied her?"

"He knew her carnally."

"That's terrible," said Doc "Do go on, please."

"I—I'll try. This man—his name was Dean Morton— was outraged. He went to the Baldknobbers and they agreed to help him go after Mantooth."

"Those are the vigilantes?"

"Yes," she said, her voice dropping to a whispery husk. "They—they rode over the border, into Arkansas. Dean's sister, her name is Caroline, gave him a piece of Mantooth's shirt she had torn off in the struggle. The dogs sniffed the material. Dean and the Baldknobbers went over the ground where Mantooth was last seen."

"And did the dogs pick up his scent?"

"Yes. They were good hounds. They tracked him for a ways, then got their noses full of pepper."

"Mantooth did that?"

"He did. Not once, but many times."

"Where is Dean Morton now?"

Val sniffed.

"Dead."

"Mantooth kill him?"

She shook her head and began to sob.

"I—I don't know. They found him in Turkey Creek, down to Hollister. Drowned."

"You must have known Morton well," said Doc awkwardly.

"I loved him," she said. "We were to be wed."

The tears came in a rush then, filling up the silence in the room.

For a long time the only sound came from the bubbling pots of water on the stove and Valerie's deep, racking sobs.

"What are you boiling water for?" Doc asked.

"Huh? Oh." She dabbed at her eyes with Doc's kerchief. "I've drawn water for my bath. This is the day I go to town. I—I forgot all about it."

"Springfield?"

"No, to Hollister. That's where Dean's buried. I usually visit his grave once a month and put fresh flowers out."

"I'm going that way," he said softly.

She looked at him with reddened eyes.

"You remind me of him," she said. "He was quiet. Right smart, too. He read a lot of books."

"You miss him."

"Yes."

Doc got up from the table and walked around to her side. He put his hands on her shoulders. She turned and lifted her head to look up at him. Then she slid out of her chair, rose up, and twined her arms around his neck. He embraced her, feeling the warm cushions of her breasts as they pressed against his chest.

She shuddered.

Doc found her lips and kissed her.

She responded willingly, eagerly.

"I—I'd better fill my bath," she said softly.

"I'll help you."

But she clung to him and kissed him warmly on the lips. Doc felt desire stir in his loins.

She broke away from him, her eyes damp with tears, and blindly reached out for cotton padded mittens. She gave him a pair and put a pair on herself.

The wooden bathtub was on the back porch. It was half full of well water. Doc poured a pot of steaming water into the tub. The water hissed as a cloud of steam enveloped him. Val poured boiling water in from the pot she held.

"The tub's big enough for two," she said, stepping away.

Her hair was damp, limp from steam. Her eyes glittered with an odd light.

"Yes. Indeed."

Val started to unbutton her shirt. He stared at her as lovely breasts tumbled into view. His crotch bulged with the sudden strain as his cock stiffened with desire.

She slipped off her shirt and tossed it on a nearby chair. She seemed to emerge from her pants as she worked them down her legs. She bent over, took off her boots, and stepped from her clothes, naked as dawn.

Doc licked his lips and removed his coat. She stepped close and helped him with his vest.

Moments later, he too was naked.

He looked at her with frank appraisal.

She was a rare beauty. Her skin was flawless, smooth. Her breasts were a pair of mature melons.

She gazed back at him, her eyes still slightly moist.

"It—it's been a long time," she said. "You must think me brazen, a heathen."

"No, Val," he said. "I just think we'd better get into that tub before the water gets cold."

He picked her up in his arms and lifted her over the side of the vat.

She slid in like a water nymph.

Doc climbed over and joined her.

She was waiting for him.

CHAPTER TEN

Raider knew he didn't stand a chance in hell of getting Beale in irons.

Not here.

This was the place Doc had named for a rendezvous, a message drop.

The Red Lion tavern.

Charlie, the bartender, knew Beale.

That meant he probably knew Mantooth as well.

"Ain't you gonna drink your beer?" asked Beale, turning to look at the undercover Pinkerton.

"Huh? Oh, yeah."

Raider brought the pail to his mouth.

"There's a glass there," said Charlie quietly. Gently.

"Yeah," laughed Beale. "You don't have to drink like a damned hawg."

Raider saw the glass and grinned sheepishly behind his bushy beard.

"Thirsty," he said. "Beer's right good, Charlie. You

known old whatzisname here a long time?"

Beale shot Raider an odd look.

Charlie, his smile noncommittal, shook his head.

"Don't know him at all. He was in here once't. Said his name was Duane. I try to 'member everybody."

"You're mighty curious, son," said Beale. "What for?"

"Oh, nothing. Just thought you two might be acquainted, the way he greeted you and all."

A sudden tension arose in the room. Raider felt it. He could have cut it with a bowie.

Charlie, as if sensing trouble, leaned over the bar and whispered to Raider.

"If you're a friend of Wagner's, in Chicago, give me the high sign."

"What's that, Charlie?" asked Beale, straining to hear.

"Nothin'. Just told the stranger to lighten up some. He seems to be carryin' a heavy load."

"Yeah, he is at that," said Beale, satisfied. "Just drink your beer, son. Don't be asking too many fool questions. I ought to be riding on anyway."

Raider nodded to Charlie when Beale's face was in the beer pail; he gave him a wink. He had to hand it to Doc. Weatherbee had handled it pretty slick. But this was not the place to jump Beale. Too many people around. If Raider was going to go undercover, no one could know that he was the one who had put Beale out of business.

Without seeming to, Raider watched Charlie with interest. Raider wondered who he was, if he was a Pinkerton or just someone Doc had sent down. The man was of medium height, gray-haired, open, rounded face, light hazel eyes. He wore horn-rimmed spectacles and an apron that could have concealed anything from a plow-handled .45 to a billy club. At any rate, the man looked as though he could handle himself.

Beale let out a loud burp.

Raider took that as a cue to leave before Beale did.

"I'll be getting me a room, Duane," he said. "Thanks for the beer."

Raider was halfway to the door before Beale replied.

"Nice riding with you," he said. "Might meet again sometime."

"I'm looking forward to it," said Raider.

He crossed the street quickly and made his way to the livery stable. He got into his saddlebags and unwrapped his .44 Remington. He checked the loads and strapped it on.

Then, in the cool shadows of the empty stable, he waited.

Across the street, the small bank was just closing. A pair of women and a man emerged and walked out of view. Raider looked at the name above the door. The Ozark Land & Trust Co. One of the clerks closed the door. A moment later a shade came down, proclaiming "BANK CLOSED."

It grew quiet on the street. Flies buzzed in the stable. The horses switched their tails and munched on grain and hay.

A half hour went by, but Raider didn't relax. He peered through the cracks in the boards.

Duane Beale came into view. He walked close to the bank, looking at it for a long time. When he turned around, headed for the livery barn, there was a faint smile on his lips.

Raider drew his pistol. He didn't cock it. This was not to be a killing.

Children played somewhere down the street. Their faint cries carried on the afternoon air.

Beale came on, unaware that Raider was waiting for him.

Raider held the pistol by the cylinder, backwards, the butt jutting out beyond his thumb and forefinger.

Beale entered the barn.

He took three paces and whirled as Raider moved in.

The Pinkerton raised the pistol butt and brought it down before Beale could turn his head. The butt smacked into Beale's skull with a sickening crunch. He dropped like a sack of meal.

Panting, Raider stood over him.

Beale didn't make a sound.

A shadow filled the doorway. Raider crouched and spun around, shifting the pistol in his hand. His thumb pushed down, cocking the hammer.

"Don't shoot," said Charlie in low whisper. "I figured you might need some help."

"Do you work for Allan?"

"Sometimes," said the bartender cryptically. "Like now." He reached in his pocket and pulled out a pair of nickel-plated handcuffs. Deftly he leaned over the outstretched body of the unconscious man and jerked his arms up behind him. Beale groaned.

Charlie slapped the cuffs on both of Beale's wrists, drew them up tight, and locked them.

"You go on now, real quick," he said. "I'll take care of this jasper."

"Who in hell are you?" asked Raider, scowling.

"Ask Doc sometime."

"Hell, you may be in cahoots with Mantooth for all I know."

Charlie stood up. He wasn't very tall; he barely came to Raider's shoulders. But he had meat in his shoulders and arms. His torso was like a barrel keg packed full of tenpenny nails. His legs were steady.

"Well, you got to take a chance. I'm going to hold this man for Weatherbee and then ship him up to Springfield. He said you might be down this way. I didn't know you'd work so fast."

"You know this man?"

"I've been working at the tavern for two months. He's been in a time or two."

"How about Mantooth? You ever see him?"

"Nope," said Charlie, dragging Beale into an empty stall. He threw a horse blanket over him. "Wouldn't know him if I saw him."

Raider swore.

"You sure as hell give a man a lot to puzzle over, Charlie."

Charlie stepped out of the stall.

"I'll be your contact with Weatherbee. If we get away with this. I'm on a ten-minute break. So far, you and I are the only ones who know you coldcocked this man."

"You don't know who he is either?"

"No. And I don't care. I was told to back you up. I figured you wanted him. You're Raider, aren't you?"

"Maybe. I still don't know who you are."

"A friend."

Raider was gone in ten minutes, but he sweated until he got out of Hollister. It had been close. He had trusted a man he'd never seen before. Maybe Doc knew what he was doing. Maybe he had set things up right, but he hadn't ought to have forgotten to mention Charlie.

Raider didn't like surprises.

Raider didn't get into Harrison until late the next evening, and he felt like he'd been riding for a year. He had done forty hard miles, and his only rest was at Bear Creek Springs, where freighters were making camp and travelers settling down for the night. He avoided them, taking his shade well away from the cluster of people staying overnight. He drank from the spring, grained his horse, and watered him without unsaddling. Now, as the lights of Harrison came into view, he remembered the note Elinore Skaggs had given him. He stopped, struck a match, and read its message. It took him five matches to get it all.

"Look up a woman named Betty Sue Summerfield," said the note in Elinore's elegantly simple script. "She may be able to help you. She lives alone on the Jasper road south of Harrison. Go to the forks where one road leads to Compton, the other to Jasper. She lives there. Tell her we're cousins and that I sent you."

The note was signed. "Love, Elinore."

There was a postscript.

"P.S. She's kin to the man you're looking for."

The hackles rose on the back of Raider's neck.

A tingle of excitement made his belly flutter.

He was getting close.

From now on, every move he made might be his last.

And his life was dependent on a complete stranger.

If he passed the next test, he thought, he had a chance.

Betty Sue Summerfield. What was she? An aunt? A spinster cousin? Elinore hadn't said. She must be pretty old to live alone. Maybe he could pass muster. One thing was sure—he'd better come up with a damned good story. If the old lady was the least bit suspicious, a trait that came natural to the old-time Ozarkers, he was a dead man.

Val giggled.

Her hands rose out of the water and stretched toward Doc's neck. He drew back in the tub, wondering if she had taken leave of her senses.

"You forgot to take off your fancy tie," she said. "Or whatever you call that piece of silk you wear around your neck."

Doc reached up and felt the ascot.

His face reddened with embarrassment.

Val's laughter echoed inside the wooden tub. She playfully splashed water in Doc's face. He tossed the damp ascot over the side with aplomb and gave her his best sportsmanlike smile.

"You're cute as a bug's ear," she said.

Doc slid toward her, feeling her naked legs under the water. Her skin was smooth and sleek as a seal's hide. She dodged around the circular wall of the tub, slithering coyly away from him.

"You little mink," he said.

She ducked under the water as Weatherbee grabbed for her. He felt something burrow into his groin. He shot halfway out of the water, startled at the intimate contact. A gob of hair floated just above his crotch. Something soft brushed against his penis. He felt a wincing shot of pleasure ripple up his spine.

Val broke the surface, droplets of water cascading off her slickened hair, her smile wide and white as a picket fence. Her hands remained below the surface, cradling his genitals, massaging his scrotum, fondling his swelling cock.

"Ummm," she hummed. "You are quite a man down there, aren't you?"

"I certainly hope so."

"Not such a dandy in the tub. I like you better this way. You don't look so much like one of those fancy advertisements in the *Harper's* magazine."

Her breasts bobbed on the water, the nipples just above the surface, floating like twin acorns. He gazed at her breasts, the perky little nubbins making little ripples in the water. Doc reached out and cupped a breast. His hand wasn't large enough to contain it. He lunged toward her and came up between the mounds like a beaver. His mouth locked on one of them. He suckled the nipple, teasing its rough surface with his tongue.

Val squirmed. Her flesh quivered with pleasure.

Doc felt her hands desperately groping him, fingers pulling on his prick like those of a milk maid.

He took her in his arms then and pulled her face to his. He kissed her wetly on the mouth and felt her hands flow up his ribs and squeeze his back. She went limp in his embrace, but her kiss was hot. His crotch throbbed with the growth of his manhood. His cock hardened like something made of iron.

"Yes, Doc," she breathed. "You are real, very real. I want you real bad."

"How?" he asked. "There's scarcely room enough for one in this wooden cage, much less two."

"There's a way" she whispered, gripping his shoulders as she nibbled on his ear. "Hold still."

She floated toward him, pulling herself close, using the buoyancy of the water to rise up and then fall into his lap. She guided herself downward until her pussy touched the crown of his cock. She held firmly onto his shoulders as she lowered herself onto his shaft, squatting with legs parted until her sex-sheath was perfectly positioned.

Doc nudged his hips upward and slid into her cunt.

Her fingers dug into his shoulder blades. She shuddered all over as she impaled herself on his swollen member.

She let out a long sigh as she sank down.

Doc began pumping upward, the water giving him a surprising bounce.

Val trembled at the onset of orgasm.

She cried out, mewing a little cry as her body quaked with the tremors of climax.

"Yes, yes," she breathed, bouncing up and down. Water splashed up on the walls of the tub.

Doc drove into her relentlessly, pounding into her quivering pussy. His blood throbbed in his temples like a sea.

She came again, her fingers digging into his back. The

water in the tub churned with the frenzy of their coupling, generating waves that enveloped them to the waist.

Doc rolled her over and pinned her against the wall of the tub. Her legs spread wider apart as Doc humped over her beneath the water. Flesh smacked into flesh, and the hot water roiled about them.

Val's mouth went slack as she spasmed again, rising up with the force of his thrusts.

"Oh, Doc," she moaned. "It's so good. I'll go with you anywhere you ask. If you want me to bring my hounds, I'll do it. Just keep fucking me."

He didn't stop until his own juices boiled.

"Yes," she wailed. "Now! Shoot your jizm in me. Fuck me, Doc, fuck me!"

Like a woman who had lost all reason, she increased her rhythm in a counterpoint to his.

Doc shot off like a cannon, shuddering with the sudden rush of pleasure.

They sank to the bottom of the tub, sated.

"Doc," she sighed, "that was wonderful. Oh, you don't have to buy a dog from me. I want to go with you. I don't care about that old outlaw. My hounds will track him down for you. Please, say you'll let me do it. I want to. For you."

"If you're sure."

"I'm sure. Please, Doc."

She wrapped her arms around his neck and peppered his face with kisses.

"All right, Val," he said, a trace of a smile on his lips. "I can use your help."

"Oh, thank you Doc. Thank you, You won't be sorry."

And Weatherbee knew he would have his manhunt without spending a penny of expense money.

CHAPTER ELEVEN

Raider wondered if he had come to the wrong place.

Lamps blazed brightly on the porch and through the windows. Horses and mules stood at the hitch rails. Wagons ringed the building.

The place looked like a town hall. Or an inn. Or, Raider decided, like a stage stop.

Men stood on the porch and sat on the steps. Others drifted in and out of the front door. He looked up at the sign hanging from the eaves over the porch: CLEMSON'S GENERAL STORE

For a moment, the Pinkerton considered that Elinore Skaggs might have sent him right onto a trap. He looked around, thinking perhaps he had his directions all wrong. But no, there was the crossroads. Road signs pointed to Compton and Jasper. The store was connected to a large house on one side, some smaller ones on the other. These were dark.

He heard voices coming from inside the store. Someone was making a speech.

As he rode up to the hitch rail, he saw that some of the men outside wore Confederate campaign hats and old uniforms. Some were drinking a clear liquid out of pint jars and smoking. The air reeked of corn whiskey.

"You a little late," said a voice. "They about done inside."

Raider said nothing. Instead, he dismounted, wrapped his reins around the rail, and walked up to the porch. Someone handed him a jar. He drank a swallow.

Fire raced down his throat. His eyes watered. A ball of lightning surged through his stomach. His breath was snatched away. Blindly, Raider reached out for something to support him—a post, a friendly arm, anything.

"You all right?" someone asked.

Raider tried to talk, but no sound came out. His scorched throat was as raw as if someone had raked it with a skinning knife.

"Likely he don't like your poison," said a man Raider couldn't see through the mist in his eyes.

"Hell, I made it last week."

"Shit. That stuff'll make you blind."

Raider gasped for air, pulling it in fast. The fire in his gut continued to blaze.

"Thanks for the swaller," he rasped, wondering if he was going to die right there.

"Y'ant another?"

Raider shook his head.

"I'm looking for Betty Sue," he said.

"She's in there, some'ers with Molly."

Raider managed to get his legs under him and climb the steps. He walked to the door unsteadily, objects swimming through a haze as he passed them. Men stood aside to let him enter.

He saw chairs set up and men lining the walls. A man stood on a soapbox in the back of the huge room.

A poster on the wall told him why there was such a crowd.

ATTENTION
— SOUTHERN PATRIOTS
COME HEAR GENERAL MANTOOTH
TALK ABOUT
IMPORTANT MATTERS
Friday Night
Clemson's
9:00 P.M.

Raider looked at the man on the soapbox. He was dressed in a Confederate uniform, complete with braid, tassels, medals, and a sword. He was tall and stood up straight. He wore a plumed hat with one side of the brim pinned up. His boots were red rough-outs, the sign of a jayhawker.

Little bumps rose on Raider's skin.

"Have you forgot the arsonist's torch that took away your homes without mercy?" shouted Seth Mantooth, his voice booming through the room. "Have you forgot the fireplace chimneys of your once't happy homes sticking up like bones everywhere across this country? I come home to smoldering ruin. I had to look for my damned farm. The Union rabble and the bushwhackers used up my rail fence for campfires."

Raider cautiously looked around the room. He noticed something curious. Most of the men wore red armbands on their sleeves. The armbands were emblazoned with a swatch of yellow cloth in the center, resembling a miniature sunburst. The men looked at Mantooth with glittering eyes, their faces mirroring their fanaticism. He had seen such facial expressions before. These were the faces of men willing to fight for their leader. These were men who had been hit hard by the war, whose homes and lives had been wrecked, who festered under the terrible yoke of injustice. These were men who would follow Seth Mantooth in order to regain their dignity—or to taste the sweet sip of revenge.

"You there, Frank," orated Mantooth. "You remember what they did to your town, Berryville. There were fifty-one houses there at the start of the war. When the Union troops were finished, all that was left was Hubbert's Hotel and two small houses. And you, Lemuel. What about Carrollton? It was the county seat of Carroll County, the most prosperous town hereabouts, with four big stores doing a thriving business, a mill, a courthouse, two big old two-story hotels, and a whole bunch of houses. When the smoke blew away, all that was left was a springhouse and two run-down stables. The whole town was gone—wiped out!"

Men shouted and raised their fists in angry remembrance.

Mantooth's gaze swept the room, picking out the faces of men he knew, men who had been hardest hit when the forces of war swept over their towns, their homes.

"Bill Sansom, there. You're from Huntsville, county seat of Madison County. What happened there in '63 when the Union butchers came through? I'll tell you what happened. The town was completely destroyed. What was left? The Masonic Lodge hall, three or hour little old houses. And we won't forget Fayetteville or Bentonville or Yellville.

"Is Sam here? Sam Bostwick. Yeah, from Dubuque down at the mouth of West Sugar Loaf Creek. Sam had a steamboat landing there, and the Federals came through and destroyed everything in their path, including the landing. That's where a lot of you were recruited into the Confederate army."

Raider listened carefully as Mantooth listed the homes and towns that were devastated during the war. He omitted the fact that some of the places he mentioned were destroyed as much by Rebels as by Union troops. However, he was making his point, stirring up the gathering with his incendiary declamation.

But why?

That was the puzzle. What did Mantooth want? What was he leading to? This kind of talk usually ended up with a mob being formed, a man being lynched. But there was no enemy here. The war was over. A long time ago.

So why was Mantooth irritating old wounds? Why was he stirring up painful memories among people who had probably lost everything and had been trying to rebuild for years?

Raider did not have long to wait. Mantooth's voice rose in pitch. His tone grew stronger, more coercive.

"Well, who in the name of Jehovah took over when the Federals and the carpetbaggers got through with you? Who bought up your lands cheap and moved you out instead of offering a helping hand? Who rode roughshod over you when all you wanted to do was rebuild your homes?"

Raider was not prepared for the chorus of voices that rose up as one, a deafening shout that reverberated like thunder in the room.

"Ozark Land and Trust!"

"Right!" shouted Mantooth, doubling up his fist.

"And are we gonna let 'em get away with it?"

"No!"

"No!"

Mantooth took a breath and rocked back on his heels. He paused, waiting for the echoes to die down, waiting for the words to sink in deep.

"Men," he said, in a confidential tone that still managed to reach the farthest recesses of the room, "I want you all to be ready. One of these days, very soon, I'm going to ask you to ride the trail of vengeance and justice with me. I promise you you'll get your lands back, your homes. Are you with me?"

"We're with you!" the crowd shouted in unison.

"When the call comes, you be ready."

"We'll be ready!"

Mantooth stepped down from the soapbox to a rousing cheer. Men slapped him on the back as he made his way through the crowd. Men that Raider had not noticed before swarmed around him like bodyguards. They began to form a wedge through the assemblage.

Mantooth walked straight toward Raider.

The Pinkerton tried to shrink into the wall, but the big man's gaze riveted on his.

There was no escape.

Raider would either pass the test or he would die.

He got a good look at Mantooth as the man approached. Raider scanned his lean hawk face, the deep-sunk eyes, black as olive pits, the hooked aquiline nose, the thick beard. He was lean, with squared-off shoulders that gave him a quasi-military bearing. His gray shirt, his gray trousers, with its single white stripe, the red rough-out boots, the plumed officer's hat, further added to his military appearance. The men with him were dressed the same, all carrying their pistols backwards, in flapped holsters that bore the embossed initials CSA: Confederate States of America. A couple of them carried Spencer carbines as well.

Mantooth stopped two feet away from Raider.

It seemed to the operative that no one breathed in the room. No one looked at him kindly. He stood out, he was sure, like a wad of tobacco in a punch bowl.

"I don't know your face," boomed Mantooth. "Who in hell are you?"

"I—uh, I come to see Betty Sue. My cousin sent me."

"Betty Sue Who?"

"Summerfield."

"Go fetch Betty Sue," said Mantooth, his voice like the whisper of a whip before it cracks across a man's face.

There was a commotion in the crowd. Loud voices. Whispers.

Mantooth stood there looking Raider up and down. Raider could almost feel his life ebbing away. Everyone nearby stared at him with equal suspicion.

The crowd parted, and two women appeared.

Both were lovely.

"Betty Sue," said Mantooth, "You know this jasper?"

She had dark hair that hung in ringlets of curls down past her shoulders. She had light blue eyes and a pretty mouth. Her nose was cut off sharp, and she had freckles on either side. Dimples. She wore a dress that was plain but didn't hide her figure. The other woman had flaming red hair, electric blue eyes, an even more ample figure.

The dark-haired one shook her head.

"Never saw him before."

"How about you, Molly?"

The redhead shook her head even more solemnly than had Betty Sue.

"Mike, come here," said Mantooth.

A young man edged into the circle.

"Is he the one you saw with Beale?"

"No. He—he's not the one."

Raider's mind worked fast. Doc had told him that Paul Stone had a man working for him named Mike O'Malley, but that he wasn't a suspect. Not then. If this was O'Malley, then Doc's life was on the barrel top if he showed up.

"You better talk fast, mister. Nobody knows you here."

Raider knew that if he showed one whit of fear he would have an ugly death. These men meant business. He thought fast, wondered if he could get by with the name Parker again.

"My name's Jess Skaggs," he said. "From over to Viola. My cousin Elinore said I might find hospitality here."

Molly Clemson stepped close, her eyes scathing in their intensity.

"You don't bear much resemblance to Elinore," she said.

Raider swallowed.

"Well," he drawled, "we ain't real close cousins."

"What you want here?" asked a man Raider did not know.

"Why, I want to join up, wear one of them armbands. Hell, we was burnt out too, same as everybody else after the Elk Horn Tavern fight. I growed up poor and mean. I can ride and shoot, and I don't like Yankees."

Mantooth stared at him blankly for a long moment and then roared with laughter, throwing his head back. After a second's pause the others began to laugh. The tension dissipated like morning fog.

"How come we never seed you before, or heard tell of you?" asked Mantooth after he recovered.

Raider tried his best to look sheepish.

"I reckon I been in a Yankee jail," he said.

"What'd you do, boy?" asked a wag. "Spit on the sidewalk?"

Raider was ready for him.

"Robbery, assault, murder."

A hush came over the crowd.

It seemed to him that Molly and Betty Sue looked at him with more respect. Certainly Mantooth took notice.

"You done all that? How come?"

"I wanted to get even."

Mantooth's expression softened. An odd light glittered in his eyes.

"You drink corn?"

"I sure do," said Raider, licking his lips.

"Well, come on, then, let's get more acquainted. I want to hear all about your one-man war against the Union."

"Bring us a jug!" said one of Mantooth's cronies.

A jug was passed up. The crowd thinned as men left the store to go to their homes. Raider felt himself being jostled along. Someone set out chairs by a wood stove, returned benches borrowed for the meeting.

"Set yourself, Skaggs," said Mantooth. Raider sat down. Men came up and took chairs nearby.

Someone pulled the cork from a jug of corn whiskey with a loud popping noise. A moment later the Pinkerton found a jug shoved into his hands. He took a long swallow to approving glances.

"He damned shore knows how to drink," said one of the men.

Raider wanted to scream. The liquor burned a path of fire down his throat, exploded in his stomach, and drenched the lining of his gut with searing lava. But he held his gaze steady and did not take a breath. He fought back tears, widening his eyes slightly. He had forgotten how strong corn whiskey could be. This was at least a hundred proof. More like a hundred and fifty. The pain didn't go away, it just spread through his bowels.

"Mighty fine," he said evenly.

"Damned right! I made it." Raider looked at the man.

"Lazarus Benteen," said Mantooth. "And this here's Mike O'Malley. And Hobie Stamper. That's Norville Clemson and his purty wife, Molly. And Betty Sue, who owns this place."

Raider nodded politely and passed the jug back to Benteen.

"Now," said Mantooth, after they had all had a taste of Benteen's poisonous firewater, "tell us all about the robberies and who you killed and all."

Raider knew his story would have to convince a bunch of men who could spot a liar a county away. Luckily, he was sure of himself. The stories he would tell would all involve men he had put in prison. He knew them well.

He looked at Betty Sue Summerfield.

There was no sympathy there, but she looked like the smartest one of the bunch. He would tell his story to her and let the rest of them weigh his words.

If he got through it, he knew, he was in.

Right square in the middle of the rattlesnake nest.

If Mantooth and the others didn't believe him, he was sure he would be swinging from a tree before the sun came up in the morning.

"Well," he said slowly, "I been in Leavenworth for nigh onto eight years. It all started when I robbed a Yankee stagecoach, the first one, about ten years ago, after I lost my mam and pap..."

The look in Betty Sue's eyes told him that he had them from the very first word out of his mouth.

CHAPTER TWELVE

Charlie wasn't there where he was supposed to be.

Doc Weatherbee stubbed out his cheroot and loosened his pistol, a Diamondback .38, in its holster.

The house was dark.

Judith stood hip-shot at the hitch rail.

Val Drews had long since gone on to Jasper to wait for Doc, her wagon loaded with a pair of bloodhounds named Lord Nelson and Admiral Farragut. A sweeter woman never drew breath, but he knew he was putting her life in danger. Still, it couldn't be helped. Someone had to track Mantooth down and bring him to justice.

An hour ago Charlie had agreed to meet Doc at this house between Turkey Creek and the White River. The house, made of stone, stood down in the flat bottom below the road.

"Charlie?"

The house was silent.

Doc stuck the butt of the cheroot in his vest pocket. Something was very wrong.

He walked out back. Charlie's horse was munching on grass, its reins trailing.

There was a wagon house a few yards away. That's where Beale was supposed to be locked up tight.

"Charlie?" Doc called again.

He heard a sound and crouched in the darkness.

A moan.

Doc cautiously approached the back of the house. A figure detached itself from the shadows.

"Doc," rasped Charlie. "Sweet Jesus, Doc, I'm hurt."

Doc rushed to Charlie and grabbed him. His hand touched something sticky on the back of Charlie's head. The man collapsed in his arms.

"Steady," said Doc, laying Charlie out flat on the ground. "What happened?"

"He—he's still here," Charlie croaked. "When you came up, he—"

Doc clamped a hand over Charlie's mouth.

He strained his ears to hear a sound. Something was moving around down in the bottom. Something he could not see.

Charlie shuddered.

Doc put Charlie's head down gently. There was blood on his own hands, he knew. Someone had hit Charlie pretty hard. But who? And where was the attacker now?

Doc leaned over and whispered into Charlie's ear.

"Is Beale still in there?"

"Unh huh. I think so. Handcuffed and in leg irons."

"Good. Who hit you, Charlie?"

"He—he was in the tavern earlier. Asking questions. Someone said his name was Stone."

Doc let out a hissing stream of air. Paul Stone. The man was as elusive as smoke, but he kept popping up. How had he found out about Beale so fast? And Charlie?

Charlie was supposed to be the perfect man in the perfect spot. No one knew about him except Raider, himself, and Beale. And now Stone, apparently. Doc knew he had something to chew on now. Charlie was, in fact, Charles Steven Jobs, a talented man who had been cashiered out of the Pinkerton National Detective Agency because of his unorthodox methods. But Doc knew him to be a good operative, a fine undercover man who knew how to assimilate himself into a company, a community, an organization, and come up with solid evidence.

Jobs had served as a spy during the war, moving freely back and forth between Union and Confederate lines. His record was so good that military men still spoke of him with awe. In one particular action, he served with uncommon distinction, although he never spoke of it himself without bitterness. Weatherbee knew the story well, and, in fact, had asked Charlie if all the facts were true.

"Yes, damn it," Charlie had said. "But both sides were wrong. Cook should have surrendered but didn't believe Kissee, and Kissee shouldn't have gunned him down."

From that, Doc surmised that Charlie had not liked his part in the war, although he had been among the best of the best.

Cook's story was typical of many that rose out of the Civil War, especially in Missouri and Arkansas. In fact, Doc had thought of using Charlie because of his familiarity with the country. No one knew Charlie, he was sure. He had been too good at his craft. But Doc could see why Charlie would not take any pride in what had happened to Alfred Cook. It was one of the saddest stories Doc had ever heard.

When the war broke out, Alfred was forty years old. He was married to Rebecca Gimlin, and they were raising their seven children on a farm near Taney City in Missouri. They held slaves, since both Alfred and Rebecca were descendants of slaveholding families. Their parents lived nearby in the Swan and Beaver Creek valleys. The Cooks prospered, and the outbreak of hostilities was a blow to them, since their sympathies were obviously with the South.

Even so, Cook did not join either side, refusing to enlist in either Price's state guards or the Confederate army. Instead, he hoped to remain neutral, believing the war would end quickly and things would return to normal. He soon learned that neutrality was impossible. Radical Unionists harassed him, drove off his stock, or slaughtered it. Even as others became refugees, Cook thought he would be better off moving to a Southern state. He packed up his family and livestock and his household belongings and moved to Marion County, Arkansas.

The peace he found there proved fleeting and temporary, as foraging parties from both armies ravaged his farm, taking what they wanted. Tempers flared as families faced starvation. Cook soon found himself in the middle of an unsolvable dilemma. During the final two years of warfare along the border it became dangerous for any man found still at home while others were fighting. Some men would be called out and shot down by a fanatic. Confederate sympathizers were hunted by the Mountain Feds, who were informants for the Unionists. Union raiders began taking notice of Cook and his pacifist neighbors, and rifle fire became commonplace on the farms in that region.

At some point during these times Cook became desperate. His family was starving, his nerves were shot. He and a dozen or so others, fearing for their safety and tired of taking abuse without retaliation, banded together to fight back. Cook was elected leader of this guerrilla group. Cook realized that there was no way they could save their families from starvation or get back the goods and stock that had been stolen from them, so they agreed to adopt the tactics of their tormentors. They became like their oppressors, going on raids against those who had robbed them, attacking Unionists north of the Arkansas border, up in Missouri.

They brought back food for their families, but the Federals took notice of them. Orders were issued that Cook's band were to be considered bushwhackers, and therefore subject to hanging if captured, or they were to be shot on sight. The Union militia sent several units against Cook, combing both sides of the border for his band. They searched from Ozark, Missouri, to the lower North Fork River. Finally, Charlie Jobs was called in and told to find Cook's hideout.

Charlie found the rendezvous site for Cook's raiders. It was an abandoned house, well off any main roads, hidden from view. The owner of the house did not know that Cook was using his house, and, before Charlie's information could be acted upon, he burned the house down while Cook and his bunch were on a raid.

Charlie was sent in again, on a lone and dangerous task. He used a number of disguises and horses and tracked Cook and his band to a cave. Here the outcast bushwhackers had a perfect hideout. The cave was halfway up a bluff, with a stone wall closing off its mouth. When the band was gone, Charlie inspected it thoroughly, finding it had a large circular room just inside the entrance that would hold thirty or forty men. There was a small passageway that made for easy entrance and exit. There were openings in the wall from which rifles could fire. Anyone charging the cave could be cut down.

Jobs made his report to Captain William L. Fenex of the 73rd Infantry Enrolled Missouri Militia. He pointed out that while the cave was both a fortress and a sanctuary, it was also a deadly trap. Once inside, there was no escape.

Charlie guided Lieutenant Willis Kissee and two dozen troops to the cave. Along the way, Kissee picked up Cook's small son, who verified the location of the cavern. Kissee deployed his men and surrounded the cave. He ordered Cook and his men to surrender. No one came out, since they knew they would be instantly shot and killed. Charlie advised that the men be treated as prisoners of war. Kissee shouted out that if they surrendered they would be so treated and would not be harmed if they gave up without a fight. He gave the men four hours to make up their minds. At the end of that time, eleven men emerged from the cave, their hands up, their weapons left inside. Cook and two others refused to surrender.

"Burn 'em out," Kissee ordered. He and his men climbed to the top of the bluff and built a huge fire out of brush on the ledge above the entrance. When it was blazing hot, they shoved the burning brush over the side, right into the mouth of the cave. The wind fanned the flames and blew the smoke inside the cavern. Cook and his two holdouts, coughing and choking, blinded by the smoke, staggered from the cave. Kissee's troops opened fire.

"They left them where they fell," Charlie told Doc.

"What about the other men, the eleven who surrendered?"

"Kissee was as good as his word. He took them back to Fenex unharmed."

Doc thought of that now.

Charlie's luck wasn't holding too well. But Doc was sure he had made the right decision when he first broached the idea of hiring Jobs to serve on this special assignment.

When Allan Pinkerton had assigned Doc and Raider to the case, Weatherbee had persuaded Wagner to put Jobs on the payroll. He gathered, from what he'd heard, that Jobs had rubbed Allan the wrong way once, embarrassing a wealthy Chicago socialite. Later, however, Charlie was vindicated when the society lady turned out to be guilty of setting up her wealthy friends for a jewel thief. But Pinkerton had refused to hire Jobs back. "The man's crude, boorish," said Pinkerton, and that was the end of it. Doc wondered if Allan even knew that Charlie was working for him. He might, because very little escaped Allan. He probably figured that Charlie was expendable.

"I'm going after him, Charlie," whispered Doc. "You stay put. Can you make it?"

"He only hit me once, but he meant to kill me. He hit hard. When you rode up, you scared him off."

Doc patted Charlie's shoulder lightly, for reassurance. But he wasn't at all certain he could make good on his promise.

Paul Stone was the big enigma in this case. He was the one man who had seemed most legitimate in the beginning. Besides Beale. Yet the more Doc knew about the case the more complex it became. Why would a legitimate freight hauler throw in with a bunch of renegades?

True, Stone had ridden with Mantooth during the war, but that had been a long time ago. He had been in the cartage business a half dozen years and had done pretty well for himself.

Every time Doc thought he had something solid, something concrete in his hand, it crumbled to powder. Paul Stone had suddenly reemerged, and from the looks of Charlie's head, he had meant to kill. Certainly he knew about Beale now. Did he also know about Raider?

One thing was certain. Paul Stone could not be allowed to get away. He knew too much. Once Mantooth found out that Beale was in custody, he'd spook like a gun-shy pup.

And Doc wanted Beale alive. He could tell them a great deal about Paul Stone and Seth Mantooth—if he could be made to talk.

Doc slipped away from the shadows of the house and headed toward the bottoms behind the carriage house. If he could put himself between Stone and Beale, he might have a chance to prevent an escape—or something worse.

The Pinkerton moved slowly, using the few standing trees for cover and taking advantage of the underbrush. This type of stalk was to his liking. He was getting his suit soiled and his shoes dirty, yet he knew that Charlie was lying back there helpless and Stone was after Beale. He had to go after Stone. He was the only one who stood a chance of stopping him.

Careful to move soundlessly, Doc reached a point near the carriage house. From this vantage point, every tree looked sinister, manlike; every shadow took on the shape of a potential enemy. Hugging the ground, Weatherbee moved behind a small oak and nestled against its trunk. He drew his pistol but did not cock it.

He waited, listening to every vagrant sound.

Something moved beyond his vision. He heard the scrape of something—a foot, a hoof—against grasses. The faint starshine dusted everything with silver, but the moon had not yet risen. Each time he looked at a suspicious shadow, the darkness seemed to deepen. Doc's eyes felt the strain; they began to burn as he sought to see his enemy, or his enemy's horse.

A thought occurred to him. Was he facing one man or two?

Doc's hand turned clammy. The pistol butt turned slick in his grasp. His throat went dry from fear. He looked over his shoulder. The little carriage house loomed dark and forbidding. What was Beale doing? Waiting? Listening?

Was he getting ready to spring from his prison as soon as Stone broke the lock? Or was he already freed?

Doc's senses shrieked with alarm as he heard a boot scrape against stone.

A moment later, Charlie groaned in pain.

Doc wanted to strangle him into silence.

Then it was quiet again, and Doc's ears seemed to roar with the sudden soundlessness.

Stone was out there. Somewhere. Somewhere close. He could sense him now, could almost feel his presence.

The waiting became unbearable. Doc thought he ought to make a move, a sound, flush Stone out. But to do this would be foolish, he knew. Maybe that's what Stone was waiting for. Doc could almost feel the man's finger squeezing the trigger of a rifle or a pistol.

In the darkness, he knew, death waited, lurking in the shadows.

The minutes crawled by and death moved in still closer, like a poisonous snake hidden in tall grasses.

Invisible, but there, nonetheless. Sniffing him out.

Getting closer.

CHAPTER THIRTEEN

The silence grew to a hammering roar in Doc's ears.

Then a twig snapped.

To Doc it sounded like his own neck. He fought down the urge to leap up and start shooting blindly, to rake the brush with lead. He forced himself to remain calm and find out where the sound had come from. Thirty or forty yards away. Off to his left.

So, he reasoned, whoever was out there was circling, trying to flank him.

Doc's skin crawled. Sweat oozed from his pores. Stone must know where he was.

Yet Doc was sure that he could not be seen. His shoulder hugged the trunk of the oak, and he presented no silhouette. Still, the man out there could have a general idea of Doc's position.

The waiting stretched Doc's nerves to their limit.

Then he had to wait no longer.

He started to scratch his eyebrow, which was sodden with sweat, when the sound of hoofbeats chewed up the silence.

A horse pounded toward him. Then the dark lightened as a ball of orange flame erupted down in the bottoms. From the sound of the explosion, Doc knew it was a pistol shot.

Charlie Jobs sat up at the sound of the gunshot. He saw the streak of orange flame; he heard the rumble of hoofbeats. He tried to shout a warning to Doc, but his voice cracked. He struggled to his feet and clawed for his pistol.

Doc fought off the urge to stand up, get out of the way of the horse, avoid being shot dead where he lay sprawled next to the oak tree. But his reason prevailed, and he held his position. The horseman had shot at him, which was unnerving enough, but the bullet whined several feet away from where he lay.

Still, he couldn't just stay there and have Stone ride right over him. As Doc prepared to return fire, another shot boomed. This time the lead ball sizzled closer and thumped into the tree Doc was using for protection. Tiny chips of wood spattered against his derby. He winced, closing his eyes for a brief second.

When he opened his eyes again, he saw the dark shape of the horse pounding his way. Doc rolled around the trunk of the tree and got to his knees. He brought his pistol up, seeking a target.

But the rider hugged the horse, presenting no silhouette.

Doc let out a soft curse.

The horse rumbled closer.

Stone fired again. This time the fire-flash was low, alongside the flank of the horse. Still, Doc had no clear target. It was either shoot the horse or risk giving Stone an insurmountable advantage.

Doc's finger tightened on the trigger. He drew a shallow breath and held it.

He squeezed the trigger. The .38 bucked in his hand. A flash of red-orange flame spewed from the barrel. The horse went down. The rider cried out and tumbled out of the saddle.

Doc rushed up as the horse thrashed wildly, a bullet in its chest. Blood gushed out of the entry wound with every pump of its heart.

The Pinkerton fired another bullet into the animal's brain. Then he straddled the downed rider.

Duane Beale brought up his pistol and took aim at Weatherbee.

Doc had no choice.

He shot Beale in the chest.

Beale's body jerked as the slug tore through ribs and a lung and blew out his back, leaving a hole the size of a tomato.

"Look out, Doc!" croaked Charlie Jobs.

Weatherbee whirled and saw the figure looming up out of the darkness. The man fired point-blank. Doc felt a bullet whiz past his face, smelled the burnt black powder, choked on the smoke. He fired into it and heard a scream.

Charlie staggered over, holding the back of his head.

He struck a match.

"Know him?" he asked Doc.

"Paul Stone, I guess. I don't know him. Never saw him."

Doc's bullet had caught Stone in the neck, right next to the windpipe. He made wheezing sounds when he breathed; blood bubbled out of his throat and streamed from the corners of his mouth. His eyes glittered in the light from the match.

"He won't make it," Charlie said.

"No. He's strangling to death now. Cyanosis is already turning his lips blue."

They both heard a loud groan and turned. Jobs tossed the match away. It sputtered out.

Duane Beale struggled to get up. Doc and Charlie walked over to where he lay.

"Better save your strength," said Doc. "Stone's just about dead."

"How—how bad?" asked Beale, his face masked by shadows. His voice rattled in his throat.

"Bad enough. You won't make it."

Charlie lit another match. He and Doc knelt beside Beale. The outlaw's face was chalk white.

"We was gonna have it all," rasped Beale.

"What's that?" asked Doc, leaning closer to Beale's mouth so he could her.

"Seth . . . Paul . . . all set up."

"What's set up?" asked Doc.

"He's babbling," said Charlie.

"Lend and take."

"Huh?"

"Paul?" Beale's face turned ashen before Charlie's match winked out. The dying man made a gurgling sound in his throat. He let out a long wheeze and then never took another breath.

Doc put two fingers to Beale's neck, feeling for a pulse. There was none.

"What was he talking about?" he said aloud.

"Damned if I know," replied Charlie. "Didn't make sense. Guess he was pretty light-headed there. Losing blood and all."

Weatherbee stood up and rammed his pistol into its holster.

Charlie got up too.

"No," said Doc. "He knew he was dying. He had something important on his mind. Something very important."

"Sounded like babble to me. Didn't make any sense at all."

Doc said nothing. Beale may not have come right out with it, but he had something weighing heavily on his mind. It concerned Mantooth and Stone, of course, and probably much more.

"Can you take care of this mess, Charlie?"

"I'm all right now. I'll take care of Stone and Beale."

Doc walked over to Stone's body again. He fished out a cheroot and sulphur match. He struck the match on the sole of his boot. In the flaring light he looked again at Stone's face. He wished now he had met the man before he had died. He lit his cheroot and tossed the match away.

He walked to the Studebaker, heavily troubled.

There were no answers yet, only more questions.

More puzzles.

Raider lazed in the easy chair, watching Betty Sue play the dulcimer. She sat curled up on a large pillow in the center of the room, her hair shimmering in the lamplight. She began to sing, her voice low and delicate. Her inflection was pure; each word was as clear as crystal.

The Pinkerton sipped from a cup of strong coffee, relieved that Mantooth and his men had apparently accepted him. They were gone now. He was alone with Betty Sue in her house, assured of bed and board until Mantooth made his next move.

Raider had heard the story of Allen Bain before, but he'd never heard it sung. It was a sad song, full of minor chords. It was a true story, he gathered, about a man who was nearly hanged for a murder he didn't commit.

"They're taking me to the gallows, Mother,
  They're going to hang me high.
  They're going to gather around me there,
  And watch me until I die.

For they say I've murdered Allen Bain,
  Or so the judge has said.
  They'll hang me from the gallows, Mother
  They'll hang me till I'm dead.

So lay me in my coffin, Mother,
  As you've often see me rest.
  With my right hand beneath my head,
  The other across my breast.

Then place my Bible upon my heart
  And, Mother, do not weep.
  Just kiss me as in days gone by
  You'd kiss me in my sleep.

My little sister Bessie will weep,
  And kiss me as I lie.
  Just kiss her twice, three times for me,
  And tell her not to cry.

Then tell that maiden that I love so well
  That I am faithful yet,
  But I must lie in a gallows grave
  And she had best forget.

Up rides a horseman on a galloping steed,
  And with a gallant rein.
  He waves his hand, he waves again . . .
  Good heavens, 'tis Allen Bain.

The dead's alive, the lost is found.
The prisoner was relieved.
He waves his hand, he waves again,
The prisoner is released.

Oh, praise the Lord, my own dear mother,
For your dishonored one.
For the murder of the gallows tree so dark
Was cheated of your son."

Betty Sue looked at Raider. Her eyes were brimming with tears.

"You sing right nice," he drawled, concealing the emotion he felt. "Real pretty."

"Oh, that old song always makes me weepy."

She put down the dulcimer and came and sat beside Raider. He did not move away. She drew her legs up under her and put a hand on his shoulder.

"Where did you really come from?" she asked.

"I told you. Viola."

"No, I mean now. Into my life. Seth was very suspicious of you. He don't take kindly to strangers."

"Elinore, she said you'd make me welcome."

"She—she's a good person. I wonder why she sent you here. But maybe she doesn't know. I reckon Molly was going to tell her but didn't get around to it."

"What's that?" he asked, interested.

"Oh, Seth will tell you when the time comes, I reckon. Pretty soon now. First time he's come out in the open with so many people in one place. But he's been talking revenge for a long time."

"Revenge?"

Betty Sue looked away for a moment and bit her underlip. Raider wanted to pry as much information out of her as he could, but he knew he was treading on dangerous ground. He had gotten in by the skin of his teeth, and he didn't want to ruin the progress he'd made.

"You saw what those damn Yankees did to us."

"Yes, but that was fifteen, sixteen years ago."

"We remember," she said bitterly. "And they're still a-doing it to us."

"Doing what?"

She sighed and moved closer.

"I forgot. You've been away. Locked up in that Yankee prison."

"Has Seth got some plan? Who is he after?"

"I—I can't say any more, Jess. Maybe I've already said too much."

"Yeah, well, I reckon Seth will tell me when the time comes."

"Oh, he likes you. I could tell that. But he doesn't know you yet. Neither do I, matter of fact. It must have been plumb lonesome in that prison."

"Yeah. Lonesome enough."

She began to twirl her fingers through his hair, then through his beard.

"I wonder what you're like under that beard. Right handsome, I'd say."

Raider said nothing.

She snuggled up next to him. Raider set his coffee cup down.

"I don't know you well either," she purred softly.

He thought of how it had been when Betty Sue had insisted he stay with her. At first he thought there was going to be trouble. The other men had looked at him darkly, and Molly Clemson had frowned. but Mantooth had laughed and said he guessed it was all right.

"Why aren't you married?" Raider asked suddenly.

"I was. Yankees come and got my man. Hanged him."

Now he knew why the song had been so sad. No one had come to rescue her husband. Now he was dead.

"What did he do?"

"Killed a Yankee."

Raider didn't ask the next question. Such a deed might not be considered murder among the hill folks who had been burned out during the war. They carried grudges a long time down this way.

He felt her lips brush against his cheek.

"I get lonesome too," she whispered. Her tongue flicked out and tapped his earlobe. He felt a sharp electric tingle. His cock began to swell with blood. "Real lonesome. Sometimes I can't stand it, it gets so bad. Malcolm, he died nigh two years ago. I wore widow's weeds for more'n a year."

"Long time."

"Yes. Too long." Her tongue slithered inside his ear, probing, wet. Raider's crotch bulged as his manhood swelled and hardened.

She didn't look deprived. But she acted like a she-wolf in heat. Before he knew what was happening, Betty Sue was in his lap, smearing his mouth with kisses, working her tongue over his lips until they felt scorched.

He touched a breast and felt its fullness.

"I'm hot," she breathed.

He grabbed her and crushed her in his arms. She squirmed around and straddled his lap. She began to move her hips, pressing against his crotch. His cock threatened to burst the buttons on his fly.

"Take me," she said. "Now."

"Now?"

In reply, she slipped out of her blouse, then, without taking off her skirt, she tore off her panties. She flung them into the center of the room and began working at Raider's trousers. She unbuckled his belt, jerked his pants down, and slipped them over his shoes. She almost ripped his shorts off in her frenzy.

She straddled his lap again, grabbed his cock, and guided it to the portal of her sex. She sank down, sighing, onto his throbbing shaft. Her fingers threaded through his hair; they took a firm grip as she pumped up and down, burying his cock deep in the moist heat of her cunt.

Raider let her have her head. He didn't need to prove anything. Betty Sue wanted it as bad as she had said, and he wasn't about to deprive her of pleasure. She began to climax but didn't let up. Up and down she bobbed, making his prick stroke her long and deep. He felt the muscles in her legs squeezing, squeezing.

"Lordy, yes!" she shrieked, and he felt her skirt flouncing against his bare legs.

He gobbled her breasts, laving the nipples with his tongue. Her back arched with pleasure, and she shuddered with a series of flesh-shattering orgasms.

"This is what I've wanted!"

Raider held on to her as she became more animated. She bounced up and down on his rock-hard shaft like a woman gone mad. Her eyes rolled in their sockets and her mouth went slack as her fervor increased.

Her skirt worked up to her hips and she gradually began to lose control of her body. She fell backwards, her body bucking with orgasms, and he lifted her up slightly and, without breaking contact, laid her flat on her back. He took the top position and burrowed still deeper, ramming hard thrusts of his cock clear to the mouth of her womb. She lifted her legs and her skirt flowed up around her waist. He saw the base of his cock nestled in the dark thatch that covered her sex-slit, the dark tangle of pubic hairs. Her breasts swelled as she arched her back again, her body shaking violently with the quake of orgasm.

And soon he could no longer contain himself or hold back the seed in his scrotum.

She gripped him tightly and squeezed him as he came, until his own spasms ceased.

A lamp died down, its wick burned short, sputtering in its last feeble attempts to flame.

The house grew quiet.

Then, in the silence, he heard the sounds of her stifled sobbing.

"Is something wrong?" he asked.

"No. I'm just happy. And sad, too."

"Why?"

"If—if Seth takes you in with him, you might—"

"Might what?" he asked.

"Die," she said.

And he wondered what Seth had planned that was so dangerous.

CHAPTER FOURTEEN

Seth Mantooth's headquarters lay in some of the roughest country in the Ozarks. Beyond Jasper, south of Harrison, the land bunched up into a place of steep, rugged hills, deep hollows, high ridges, thick with densely packed trees, hardwoods and cedar, redbuds, dogwoods, tangled underbrush. Beyond a little community called Deer was a place even less populated, for it lay in low, rugged country, surrounded by natural fortifications of sheer bluffs and majestic rock-strewn mountains. The few people in the region called this place Limestone, but few had been down in its flat, hemmed-in valley since Mantooth had set up his hideaway there. A little creek ran across the bottoms, fed by springs. There was plenty of water, wild game, and an entrance road that could be easily defended with a handful of men.

The outlaw and his band had been there a week since the big meeting at the crossroads in Harrison, laying out the strategy for the days to come. During this time there had been no raids and no word from either Stone or Beale.

The disappearance of these two key men was a puzzling mystery to Mantooth. He didn't like it a damned bit. He had been snarling most of the week.

Now, early of a morning in midsummer, sitting on the porch of the big cabin, with the the meadowlarks piping in the large field that sprawled beyond the cluster of log buildings, he chewed on a cut plug of Climax tobacco. A scowl was etched into his face.

"I don't like it none," he told Lazarus Benteen. "Beale's way overdue. Expected him about the time that jasper Jess Skaggs showed up."

"Clemson went right on up there to check, to backtrack Beale."

"And what about Paul Stone? Where in hell did he go to?"

"He said he was going to Forsyth to meet Duane. I reckon he didn't find him. Or the two of 'em went fishing."

Mantooth spat a stream of brown tobacco juice off the edge of the porch. He wiped his lips of stain.

"Somethin's fishy, all right," he said.

"Maybe Beale didn't come through Forsyth," ventured Hobie Stamper, his back to the cabin wall, his knife whittling idly away at a stick of green oak. "Maybe he come through Hollister."

"Might have," said Benteen. "If so, Paul would've gone over there when Duane didn't show in Forsyth."

"That's what he said he'd do," agreed Stamper.

Mantooth's looked continued sour.

"We can't wait on 'em. Maybe the Pinkertons caught 'em up."

"Not them," said Hobie. "Paul's too smart. Duane's too mean."

Benteen nodded in agreement.

Seth looked up the road and cocked his head. He stood up and spat tobacco juice into the dirt. There was the sound of a horse galloping, then the clear notes of a bobwhite quail.

"Boys, here comes Molly. Let's get saddled. We're short a man or two, so we're going to give that Skaggs a test. You keep your eye on him. He does anything wrong, you put out his lamps."

"You going to . . ." said Hobie.

"Molly wouldn't be here if the next freighter coming down to Carrollton wasn't carrying something we need. Hobie, you set out some grub for her. Laz, you put Molly's mount away and fetch up our horses."

Moments later Molly Clemson rode up, her red hair flying. Her horse was lathered with foam, his hide sleek.

"Trouble?" asked Seth.

"Maybe," she panted, struggling for oxygen.

"Get your breath, then tell me what you know."

He helped Molly dismount. Lazarus took the reins of her horse and walked him down to the stables. Molly stood there a moment, holding her side, her mouth working like a fish's out of water. Seth helped her to the porch and sat her down.

"Day after tomorrow there'll be a freighter coming into Carrollton carrying dynamite, cash for the ginseng pickers."

Seth smiled.

"The drovers will be armed, and they'll have outriders."

"How many?"

"Five outriders. A driver and a shotgun."

"You done good, Molly. How come you to wear out a horse getting here?"

"Saw Norville up at the store. He just come from Hollister."

"So?"

"He says that two pine boxes went out of there to Springfield two days ago. Paul and Duane."

Mantooth swore.

"What happened? Who killed them?"

"Nobody knows. A U.S. marshal came down with the boxes and carted 'em off."

"How's your husband?"

"Scared. He says to tell you that it looks like open season."

"You rest up, Molly, then get back to Carrollton and set things up. We're taking the new jasper along."

"Skaggs?"

"Yes. You see him?"

"I saw him. He and Betty Sue hit it off right well." Seth thought he detected a trace of bitterness in her voice. "She's got him fixing up the henhouse and crawling over the roof patching holes."

Mantooth laughed.

"She needs a man."

"Who doesn't?" snapped Molly before she could stop the words.

Mantooth turned away, embarrassed. He knew her marriage with Norville wasn't good. And now it seemed he was turning into a yellowback.

"You set things up," he said, stalking off. "Hobie's settin' out grub for you. Send him down when you go in."

Molly nodded. She watched Mantooth walk away, wondering what made him so hard. Inside, her stomach was fluttering. All she could think about was Paul Stone and Duane Beale. Dead. And those other men up at the Springfield office. She didn't know them, but she knew that Seth had blown them to pieces with dynamite.

She shuddered to think what he might do to anyone who crossed him.

* * *

Raider had to hand it to Mantooth—he didn't miss a trick.

Benteen and Clemson, bandannas pulled up over their faces, waited on either side of the narrow passage, flanking the road, out of sight behind the hill that had been split in two by dynamite when the builders came through. He and Hobie were well off the road, ready to close the door once the freighter went through and was stopped by Benteen and Clemson.

Mantooth waited atop the hill, concealed behind a large oak. His big Tennessee Walker horse was tethered out of sight in thick brush. Seth had a glass and was squinting into it, gazing toward Alpena. Carrollton was south, and the road was clear.

All Raider knew was that they were going to rob a freighter and he was expected to do his part. He could almost feel all the men's eyes on him.

He looked up at Mantooth.

As if sensing this scrutiny, Seth returned the look.

Raider felt the outlaw's eyes burning into his own.

The bandanna over his face was suffocating. Sweat dripped into his eyebrows and smeared his back.

The minutes crawled by. Hobie Stamper, across the road, held a rifle at the ready. He and Raider were the rear flankers, with orders to let the wagon pass into the gap, then ride up fast when they heard Clemson and Benteen open fire. Mantooth would cover them all from his position atop the ridge.

It was a slick plan, if all they had to worry about was a wagon and two men. Raider wondered. Doc had told him that many of the freighters were beefing up security, sending along outriders to make certain the shipments got through.

He heard the rumble of a wagon, the pounding of hooves. When he looked up, Mantooth was giving the signal. A moment later he disappeared. Across the way, Hobie drew back out of sight. Only the snout of his rifle poked through the brush.

Raider backed his horse up into the thicket.

The sounds of the approaching horses grew louder.

The Pinkerton knew that there was more coming than just a wagon pulled by two horses. He knew also that he was in a peculiar position. He couldn't shoot down men during a robbery. While he must play an undercover role, he would have no legal defense for what was tantamount to murder. Some instinct told him that this was some kind of test. If he failed it, he had no doubt that Mantooth would either kill him personally or have him killed.

He drew his rifle from its scabbard, hoping that he could pull it off without killing anyone and without arousing Mantooth's suspicions.

The first outrider rode into sight. He glanced around without stopping, then continued on past Raider and Stamper. Two more riders came into view. They stopped and waited for the freight wagon to catch up. A few seconds later the wagon appeared, flanked by two more riders.

Raider watched the wagon go through the pass and waited for the first gunshot. Instead, one of the riders dropped back and turned around. He rode straight for Raider as the wagon slowed to a stop.

Something had made the rider suspicious, Raider surmised. He tensed as the lone rider drew closer. The guard levered a round into the chamber of his rifle.

"What's up?" someone called.

"Thought I saw something," said the approaching rider.

Then all hell broke loose.

Hobie Stamper fired first. The explosion ripped through leaves and branches. The man on horseback stiffened. A hole appeared in his chest. A crimson stain spread over his shirt. The rifle slid from his hands. Then a series of explosions boomed in the pass. Dust and smoke filled the air. Men shouted and cursed.

"Come on!" yelled Stamper, riding out of the brush.

Raider touched spurs to his horse and rode into the pass behind Stamper. Bullets whistled all around. He saw the shotgunner jump down from the stalled wagon, whirl, and crouch. The guard fired the sawed-off Greener, and the gun roared. The air filled with orange flame and the angry whine of buckshot pellets. A second later, Mantooth rode up behind the shotgunner and fired point-blank into the back of his head. The guard crumpled.

Stamper's horse caught the full load of buckshot and went down, blood gushing from a dozen wounds. Hobie was thrown from the saddle.

To Raider's surprise, one of the outriders turned his horse and rode straight for the Pinkerton. Gunfire erupted from rifles, but the rider lay flat on his horse's back. He did not fire at Raider but rode on past, clapping his spurs into the flanks of his mount, hell bent for leather.

"Shoot that man!" yelled Mantooth.

Stamper rolled over in the dirt, groping for his rifle. He shook his head groggily and tried to sit up.

The rider almost ran him down, then zigzagged at the last moment.

Raider raised his Winchester '73. He fired well above the head of the retreating rifle.

Behind him, three shots rang out in quick succession. The driver of the wagon tumbled from the spring seat, dead before he hit the ground. Another outrider, trying to scramble for high ground, took two bullets in the back.

The escaping rider rode straight for Alpena, the way they had come, as if by prearranged plan. Raider kept firing at him, making sure all his shots went wild.

"You missed him!" accused Stamper, who was still searching for his rifle.

The last outrider went down in a hail of lead. The one that got away disappeared over the hill unscathed.

Mantooth rode up to Raider, his face flushed with anger.

"What the hell happened here?" he roared.

"I reckon one got away," said Raider.

Stamper staggered to his feet and wobbled over, a sheepish look on his face.

"I couldn't get to my rifle fast enough," he explained. "Damn Yankee shot my horse right out from under me."

Raider looked over at the dying horse. Stamper's rifle barrel jutted out from underneath its haunches.

He pointed to it. Stamper hobbled to the horse and jerked the rifle out by the muzzle.

Mantooth waited until the hoofbeats died away before he said anything.

"We'll, he's going for help," he said. "There'll damn sure be a posse on our tail." He licked dry lips and looked Raider square in the eyes. "Mister," said Mantooth, "you're the worst damned shot I ever did see in my life . . . unless you missed him on purpose."

Raider returned the look.

"I—I've been out of practice some," he said simply.

"Oh yeah. You been in prison. I forgot."

Raider said nothing.

"Well, come on," said Mantooth, slightly mollified. "Let's get what we come for and hightail it out of here. There'll be men swarming all over us pretty damned quick."

Raider beckoned to Stamper.

"Climb up behind me," he offered. As Stamper came toward him, he aimed his rifle with one hand and fired a shot into the head of Stamper's dying horse. The horse twitched several times and then was still.

"That's better," said Mantooth.

Raider grinned behind the outlaw leader's back.

Stamper put his foot in one of the stirrups and climbed up behind the cantle. Raider rode back to the wagon, where Benteen and Clemson were already at work, searching for booty. Benteen threw down a money satchel. Mantooth caught it and hooked it over his saddle horn. As if by a signal, the men began to pull down their bandannas. There was no longer any need for them. The dust settled in the pass, and the bluebottles started to swarm over the dead men and Hobie's horse.

"Cut yourself out one of those team horses, Hobie," ordered Seth, "and throw your saddle on it. Be quick. We ain't got much time."

Stamper jumped down and ran to the team. He drew his knife and began cutting the traces.

Clemson checked all the downed men, making sure they were all dead. Raider winced as Norville dispatched one of the outriders with a single bullet to the brain. He was powerless to help without revealing his true identity. He was glad now that he had grown the thick beard. It hid the look of anger on his face. If Doc had been with him, he probably would have started shooting the outlaws down beginning with Seth Mantooth. Instead, Raider forced himself to remain calm. He had to find out what the outlaws were up to, where their hideout was, and how they managed to make all of their getaways. Right now, with Alpena so close, he knew it wouldn't be long before a posse came riding after them.

Absentmindedly, Raider counted the dead men. Three outriders, the driver, and the man riding shotgun.

One man had gotten away. That he knew.

"You get them all?" asked Raider when Clemson came up to the wagon.

Clemson shook his head.

Mantooth looked at Raider.

"You don't know, do you?"

"Know what?"

"They had five outriders. And they knew their business. The minute we opened fire, one lit a shuck for Carrollton, the other for Alpena. You let your man get away."

"What about yours?" asked Raider.

Clemson and Benteen exchanged glances.

"Between the scattergun and four rifles, we were pinned down long enough for him to get away," said Mantooth. "We never got a shot at him."

Benteen untied some ropes and pulled back the canvas tarp that covered the wagon bed. He began to pry open a box. Raider rode up close, wondering what the contents of the carton was.

"How much of this you want, Seth?" asked Clemson, climbing up to help Benteen.

"Much as we can carry. Watch it. Don't get that slick stuff on your hands. You'll have a headache for a week."

"Yeah, I know," said Lazarus.

Raider's stomach knotted up.

He knew now what the outlaws were after.

Benteen grinned, slipped on a pair of gloves that had been sticking out of his back pocket, and reached into the box. He pulled out two handfuls of long, round objects. The cardboard cylinders were slick with wax.

Dynamite.

CHAPTER FIFTEEN

The crowd, which was gathered around the wagon, jostled for position. Women in sunbonnets cooled their faces with paper fans. The men stood awkwardly in the shade, wiping sweat from their necks with colored kerchiefs. Little children stared up in wide-eyed wonder at the funny man in the derby.

"If your throat is sore from damp evenings, tie the skin of a black cat around your neck. Yessir, that's what they say. Am I right? And if your skin is turning yellow, why then, roll a live spider in butter and eat it."

Doc Weatherbee paused in the midst of his spiel for effect. He stood taller than the crowd, on an oblong wooden carton. Some of the women cringed. The children giggled and made funny faces. The men rammed each other with furtive elbows.

"And, you put kerosene in the chickens' drinking water to keep them healthy in the wintertime, and you men over there, don't lie, you carry rattlesnake rattlers in your hatband

133

to cure a headache. When you worm your horses, you have to feed them chewing tobacco to get them to swallow it. Well, sir, ladies and gentlemen, I have here in my hand an elixir that will do something for everyone, even for horses, cats, dogs, goats, and chickens."

Doc paused for effect, knowing he had his audience.

He held his arm out straight, the bottle of patent medicine at arm's length so that all could see.

"When your chickens are pecking at each other, you paint the windowpanes red so when the sun shines through it'll look like they're all bloody. You there, madam, I'll bet you've carried a raw potato to rub on your arthritic joints when the rheumatiz gets to acting up. And you there, did you ever turn your shoes upside down under the bed when you went to sleep? Bet you did, to get rid of the leg cramps."

The women and children tittered as Doc looked each one in the eye. He fixed his gaze on an old-timer leaning against a shade tree.

"You there, sir, did I hear that you treat snakebite by drinking all the whiskey you can hold? Well, you don't have to get drunk when the copperhead bites you anymore. And you, young man, when you get a sty, does your ma cut the eyes out of a potato and bury them?"

The boy laughed and hid his face in his hands.

"You've all been living in the dark ages of curatives," intoned Doc with all the suavity of a carnival pitchman and all the showmanship of a Shakespearean actor. "Modern medicine has come to Alpena. Here, in this tiny bottle, is the bitter white substance from the pulverized bark of the cinchona tree, a sprinkling of purple foxglove, and other miraculous ingredients too esoteric and exotic to mention. But Doc Weatherbee's Healing Elixir will cure your rheumatiz, take away your headaches, dry up your sties, cure snakebite, make your chickens stop pecking one another, and your horse will swallow this and whinny for more."

"How much?" asked a gruff-voiced man.

"Usually I charge a dollar for this special elixir, sir, but since you all look like good folks, healthy as sin, I'm making a special offer of fifty cents a bottle. That's four bits, mister, and a better bargain you won't find between here and the Arkansas River."

Some of the women stepped up and began opening their purses. A man came up and tossed Doc a fifty-cent piece. Weatherbee caught the coin deftly and tossed the man a bottle.

"Better buy two," he said heartily.

Doc's patter hid his concerns. He had come to Alpena too late to intercept the freighter going through that morning. Four days ago he had rendezvoused with Val Drews in Jasper. They had failed to learn anything down there, although Doc had sold thirty bottles of his harmless "elixir," which consisted of little more than water, lemon juice, whiskey, various herbs, and aspirin. It wouldn't cure anyone of anything more serious than a headache, but it wouldn't kill anyone either.

He had gotten on the telegraph in Harrison and had communicated with Wagner, who told him that messages were waiting for him in Springfield. The wires had brought news of the freighter and its cargo. Sheriff Wales, still too bunged up to come down, had nevertheless helped hire the outriders and given them instructions. A posse was waiting in Carrollton and one in Alpena, in case there was trouble. From his position in a field next to a small creek, Doc could see the men waiting at the post office, their horses standing hip-shot in shade.

Val and her dogs were playing in the creek. The small crowd had come in response to Doc's noisy entrance into the town.

Maybe, he thought, the freighter had gotten through.

There had been no word from Raider in more than a week. Two days ago, Doc had ridden to Hollister and checked with Charlie.

Judith was about worn out from all the traveling. The children had taken to the mule, though, and given her sweets.

A few people bought bottles, but some hung back. Doc exhorted the fainthearted with more of his unpatented bull.

"No more will you have to smear tar on your skin to cure eczema," said Doc, holding a bottle of his "medicine" high overhead, as if it were something truly miraculous. "No more will you have to drink strong alkali water to cure obesity by warding off hunger pangs. No more will you have to put leeches on your temples to cure glaucoma." He looked into the face of a puzzled woman and said, as if in an aside, "That's blindness, ma'am, caused by a film growing over your eyes."

He strode back and forth atop the wooden carton he stood on, waving the bottle triumphantly now.

"No more bloodletting for acute bronchitis, headache, insomnia, pleurisy, sunstroke, or the ague. No sir! Doc Weatherbee's elixir will cure barber's itch, meteorism, fatty heart, softening of the brain, the grippe, griping, groping, groaning, grating, grinding, and after-pains."

He got his laugh and sold five more bottles of "medicine."

Then someone shouted.

The men at the post office grabbed for their horses.

Doc looked up and saw the lone rider approaching the curve where the Carrollton road swung into Alpena. He was still a long way off, but coming fast.

"That's all, folks," said Doc hurriedly. "Looks like trouble on a fast horse."

The people all turned and saw the rider in the distance. The women murmured; men grunted. The crowd began to break up as Doc looked over toward the creek. He saw Val and waved her in, then stepped down from the carton on which he stood. Quickly he overturned the carton and began taking bottles from the little display table. He packed them amid the clusters of excelsior, hefted the box, and shoved it into the back of the wagon. He folded the display table and crammed it in as well.

The rider slowed as the posse men mounted their horses and began milling in the middle of the road. Doc, on foot, raced behind the others, who streamed toward the post office to hear the news. Behind him he heard the baying of Val's hounds.

"What happened?"

"Who's that a-coming?"

A half-dozen voices asked a half-dozen questions before the rider was halfway there. Doc craned his neck to see the man riding up; he shaded his eyes with the curly brim of his derby pulled down low on his forehead.

"That's Jim White," said a posse man, standing up in his stirrups. "You can bet they run into trouble."

The man slowed his horse at the edge of the throng. The animal was foamy with sweat and breathing hard. The man, too, was out of breath; he could hardly speak.

"Where'd they hit you, James?" asked a man, taller than the others, atop a rangy steel gray.

"Yonder—'bout three, four mile out."

"You didn't get to Carrollton."

"No," gasped White. His face was chalk from exertion. He grasped his side in pain.

"How many?" asked another man.

"Five or six."

"Recognize any of 'em?"

White shook his head. He was young, dark-haired.

"There was a lot of shooting. Strunk, he went down. Bill

Bragg, he plugged one of their horses with buckshot. God A'mighty, they might all be dead." White's voice hung to the edge of hysteria. His eyes bulged in their sockets.

"You done good, son. We'll take it from here."

"Goin' back with you," said White. "Just let me get my breath. Somebody bring me a fresh horse."

Doc didn't wait around to hear the rest of it. He turned on his heel and interecepted Val and her dogs.

"Come on," he said. "Maybe we can pick up a scent."

"You can't outrun that posse," she said.

"No need to. If your dogs can follow a hot trail, we'll be there in less than an hour."

"They can do it," said Val.

Doc was thinking about that outlaw horse that went down. He hoped it would have enough of its rider's scent to give the dogs something to sniff.

Before the posse left Alpena, Doc was on his way, driving Judith with a relentless whip.

Raider had never seen men ride like these renegades. They didn't hurry, but they ate up the ground like locusts.

Before they reached Carrollton, Mantooth called a brief halt.

"Four bits says there's a posse waiting for us in Carrollton," he said.

"In advance?" said Norville Clemson incredulously.

"Maybe," said Mantooth. "Ready to ride. One of those outriders tried to run for Carrollton. Made me suspicious after that other one got away to Alpena. They're after us, boys, settin' the traps. We just got to keep bein' smarter'n they are."

Mantooth looked over the country. There were fields and hills with little roads winding through.

"What you thinking, Seth?" asked Hobie Stamper.

"About how long it'll take a posse from Alpena to get this far." He looked at Raider. "Skaggs," he said. "If we get separated, you stick with Hobie and you'll be all right. Otherwise you'll get plumb lost and you're liable to get shot up good."

"I understand," said Raider.

"You make sure you ride with Hobie, no matter what," Seth emphasized.

"Where?"

"Wherever he rides."

Mantooth led the men off the main road and down through fields and pastures to side roads. His route was a bewildering maze to Raider, made even more complicated by the odd configuration of the Ozarks terrain, with its hollows and hills all seemingly scrambled by some giant hand.

Raider didn't much like the idea of being dependent on Hobie Stamper, but he had no choice. He was soon lost. Mantooth rode through small creeks, hiding his trail, killing his scent, through hollows thick with brush, over hills, down steep slopes, next to sheer bluffs. Sometimes they passed close to a farmhouse and Mantooth would wave. When Raider looked back, he saw people brushing out the outlaw tracks. No wonder, thought Raider, that people had said the robbers often disappeared into thin air.

The Pinkerton operative tried to mark their direction by the sun, but Mantooth made so many twists and turns that Raider knew he could never trace their path again, even if he looked at a map. At some point in their journey Mantooth rode on ahead with Clemson and Benteen. At first Raider paid no attention to the increasing distance between him and Mantooth, but as he and Hobie rode over a ridge and kept on riding, he soon realized that Seth and the other two men had disappeared.

Raider slowed his horse.

"Where's Mantooth?" he asked Stamper.

"Gone," said the outlaw laconically.

"Shouldn't we try to catch up?"

"Nope. We done passed him anyway."

Raider reined up and looked around. All he saw was a farmhouse, a barn, some empty fields. No sign of Mantooth. Three men just swallowed up.

Hobie halted and regarded the bearded man. He began to grin.

"Don't see 'em nowheres, do you?"

Raider shook his head.

"Ain't supposed to. Come on. We got a ways to ride."

Raider looked back at the peaceful scene until it faded from view. He was sure that Mantooth hadn't been that far ahead to have ridden to the barn or house, yet he had vanished in the middle of a farm just the same. It was very puzzling.

Hobbie now seemed to be riding with a definite purpose in mind. The roads seemed to get rougher and go deeper into the hills. Much of the time they rode in shade, between steep hills, under leafy oak trees.

Soon they saw another farmhouse. Instead of skirting it, as Raider had thought they would do, Hobie rode straight for it. The house was at the edge of a field. Behind it the hills rose up in a gentle sloping. Far above, steep, craggy bluffs brooded over them like ancient monuments carved out of sandstone.

"Follow me," said Hobie. He rode toward the hill in back of the house.

Stamper hauled in on his reins some thirty yards from a grove of trees.

"Get your personals," he ordered. "Just leave your horse where it stands."

Raider watched as Hobie dismounted and took his sad-

dlebags full of stolen dynamite and took his rifle out of its
scabbard and slung them over his shoulders. The Pinkerton
shrugged and followed suit.

"Just leave our horses here?"

"Yep. Foller me."

Hobie walked toward the grove of trees and on through
them. There, on the bottom of the hillside, was a door.
Raider had seen such places before. When the pioneers from
Kentucky and Tennessee had come to the Ozarks they had
often hollowed out places in the hillsides where the water
seeped down from the bluffs. This was where the home-
steader stored his meat. It was usually cool and dank in the
man-made cavern. Later, some of the people enlarged these,
shored them up with timber or plastering, and put in their
women's fruit and vegetable jars and used them for storm
cellars. When tornado weather hit, the farmers and their
families would go to the springhouse/storm cellar and hole
up until the dangerous weather passed.

Hobie opened the door and beckoned to Raider.

Inside there were shelves loaded with jars of "canned"
vegetables, fruit, and fish. There were bunks, a table, lamps,
catalogs, a Bible, and some old newspapers. Hobie gently
lowered his saddlebags to the earthen floor and lighted a
lamp. Raider looked up and saw a tin stovepipe which
allowed air and light into the cellar. He put his things down
as Hobie turned up the wick.

"You can shet that door," Stamper said.

Raider closed the door. He looked out through a crack
and saw the horses standing outside with their ears perked.

Curious, he watched as someone came up, took the horses'
reins, and began leading them away.

"Is that"—Raider strained his eyes—"Molly I see out
there?"

Hobie laughed.

"I reckon. We'll have fresh horses in the barn, all saddled up, come morning."

Raider stepped away from the door. Hobie lay on one of the bunks, his hands behind his head.

"What is this place?" asked Raider.

"Underground railway."

"Huh?"

"This is where they hid out the slaves escapin' to the North."

Raider let out a low whistle. So this was how Mantooth and his band had managed to elude pursuit. He could see it all now. These springhouses were ready-made hideouts. Once used to hold slaves on their journey to freedom, they now were used by thieves and outlaws.

One part of the puzzle was solved, but Raider couldn't do a damned thing about it.

Yet.

CHAPTER SIXTEEN

Lord Nelson and Admiral Farragut sniffed the carcass of the dead horse.

"At least he didn't sprinkle no pepper this time," said Val, holding onto the leashes of the two bloodhounds.

"You think they can pick up the scent of the rider?"

"They sure can. That's what they're doing now."

The dogs made frantic circles around the scene of the robbery. The posse had long since gone on. The wagon, with a single horse still hitched to it, stood silent as Doc examined the ripped-open boxes. He knew now that Mantooth had stolen dynamite as well as money.

"Can those bloodhounds follow a man on horseback?" asked Doc.

"Sure. These dogs have the most powerful noses in the animal kingdom. They can pick up the scent of a man on horseback, all right. If a rider brushes against a tree, or a leaf on a branch, they can smell his scent that high up. Higher, even."

"Hard to believe."

"These dogs here have sniffed out men in barns, in trees, even in caves twenty feet or more up a bluff."

Doc was amazed. He watched them work, though, believing that they were recording and analyzing the various scents of the men who had been there. Still, he wondered, after looking over the country, if these dogs could track over such rough terrain. He was not convinced, despite Val's insistence on the power of the dogs' noses, that they could follow a man atop a horse.

Val spent considerable time at the dead horse, letting the dogs sniff its back, where the saddle marks still showed. Finally she told Doc her hounds were ready.

"Will they follow the right tracks now?" asked Weatherbee.

"We'll soon see. I imagine the posse went on to Carrollton. I'll tell you one thing, though. We'll never track Mantooth and his men with this mule and your wagon. He and his men won't be on the main roads much. We'll need good horses."

Doc considered it.

"Can we rent horses in Carrollton?"

"I know a man there who raises some stock. We'll ask him."

Two hours later, Doc, decidedly out of his element, was riding across fenceless hills on a six-year-old gelding, following Val Drews, who rode a ten-year-old bay mare. Inside his coat he carried a shirt that Raider had left with him. It might come in handy. The hounds hadn't made any mistake so far. They weren't following the posse, which had scattered all over the country looking for sign. But the posse had stayed to the roads. The hounds were ranging across broad fields and staying to ridges. The tracks Doc saw confirmed that the sniffing hounds were indeed following horses carrying considerable weight that had passed through not long before.

Val's friend in Carrollton had not only agreed to lend two of his horses to them but promised to take care of Judith and keep the medicine wagon under cover. What's more, he had agreed to drive the wagon to Hollister and meet Doc there in three days, when Weatherbee would return his horses. All this for two dollars cash money. Doc was relieved, because he had sensed an innate honesty in the man. Doc was assured by his demeanor that he wasn't sympathetic with Mantooth, or any outlaw for that matter. He had taken Val's word that Weatherbee was on the side of law and order. The two men had shaken hands. The man's name was Rule Usrey. He was thin, wiry, and as tough as a hickory stump. He looked, Doc thought, like one of those men who was at home in the rugged hills, undefeated despite many disasters, both natural and man-made.

Now, following the hounds, Doc appreciated the gentle horse under him. He much preferred traveling by train or wagon, but there were times when he was forced to fork a horse just like Raider. He wondered now where Raider was and how he had fared.

The dogs, their wrinkled faces noncommittal as mud piles, moved over the ground with hunched shoulders, their noses pulling in scent. Val held up, watching them with interest.

"What's the matter with them?" asked Doc.

"There were five men in a bunch. Now they've split up. The dogs don't know which way to go."

"So now what?"

"That's up to you. Which bunch do you want them to follow? Two men are heading in one direction, the other three seem to be angling south."

Doc looked around him. He was completely lost. All he saw were hills and more hills. A feeling of claustrophobia assailed him.

"Which way is which?" he asked.

Val pointed.

"That way, where the two men are headed, is Batavy." She meant Batavia. "Likely, they'll go through Capps to Harrison."

"And the other way?"

Val squinted.

"Rough country. Goes to Jasper. The hard way. Take us three or four days overland, at least."

"I don't have that much time."

Val shrugged.

"It's easy then. Besides, those tracks leading south I've seen before. They'll split up again, if it's like before, and my dogs will wind up with stickers in their noses."

"We'll follow the ones going to Batavia."

"We probably won't find Mantooth going that way."

Doc had a hunch, however.

"Maybe we'll find someone who knows where he went, though."

Val got the dogs started on the right track.

"One of the men ahead is the one who was riding the horse that was killed," she said.

"How can you tell?"

"Look at Nelson and Farragut. They're moving."

It was true. The dogs seemed hot on the scent. There had been times when the escaping riders had ridden through streams and Doc was sure they would lose the trail, but the bloodhounds had picked scent up out of the air or off the trees. They had lost some time, but the hounds always found the spoor again.

Now it was late afternoon and the sun was setting.

"Can we wait until morning?" Doc asked.

"Best to stay on it. Besides, I think the men we're following will run for cover."

"How do you figure that?"

"That's the pattern."

And so it was.

Late in the afternoon the dogs rushed up to the hidden springhouse and began pacing back and forth, yapping and growling.

"That's where they are," said Val in a whisper.

Doc assessed the situation.

"Sure?"

"The dogs are."

"Call them off."

"What?"

"I want them to smell something."

Val called the dogs in by whistling in a special way.

"Now let's ride off, out of sight," said Doc.

They looked at the barn and farmhouse and rode up to a ridge among trees.

"This is good," said Doc, dismounting.

Val got down. She called the dogs over.

"Make sure they're real quiet," said Doc.

She patted their heads and spoke soothingly to the two hounds. They seemed to enjoy the affection. Doc slipped Raider's shirt from under his own.

"Now give them this," he said. "See if they respond."

Val took the shirt and shook it out. She spoke to the dogs. They sniffed the shirt, then became animated. They started back off the ridge.

"Call them back," said Doc.

Val whistled.

"Would you say," he asked, "that one of the men down there is the owner of that shirt?"

"Sure would."

Doc drew a breath and fished in his vest for a cheroot. He struck a match and lit it.

"What now?" asked Val.

"Just lay back here and wait. The two men we were following are in that dugout, right?"

"Yes. The dogs say they are."

"Mind sleeping on the bare ground?"

"I've done it before."

"Good. Now if those dogs could bring us a rabbit, we could eat."

"I'm not hungry," said Val, snuggling up close to him. "But I could eat you."

Maybe it wouldn't be so bad sleeping out, thought Doc. And he wasn't hungry either. At least not for food.

"What the fuck's that?" grumbled Stamper, rising groggily off the bunk.

Outside, the bloodhounds snarled and growled. The hackles rose on Raider's neck.

"Dogs."

"Oh, shit, they sicced the godammned bloodhounds on us."

Both men went to the door and peered through the slits. Raider's heart sank.

A hundred yards away, Doc Weatherbee sat on a rusty sorrel gelding. With him was a woman, a stranger, on a big bay mare.

"Why, that's Val Drews. With some city slicker."

Raider stepped away. He was ready to put Stamper down if he made a wrong move.

"I ought to drop the sonofabitch where he is."

Raider tensed.

Stamper turned and looked at Raider.

"Fetch me my rifle, Skaggs."

"Fetch it yourself."

"What the hell's wrong with you?"

"I ain't killin' no woman."

"Me neither. It's that slicked-up dude I want to drop. He looks like city law to me."

Raider shrugged. The dogs were making a lot of noise. He couldn't let Hobie shoot Doc. He wondered what Doc was doing there, following bloodhounds. He was about to mess up everything, like he always did.

"Look, Hobie, better wait and see if he's part of a posse. Maybe we don't stand a chance."

"That's all you know."

They both heard the whistle and went back to the door.

"Be damned," said Hobie. "She's a-callin' 'em off."

Raider watched as the dogs responded to their mistress's whistle. In a few moments Doc and Val Drews rode away toward a far ridge.

Stamper turned away from the door.

"I don't like it none. Wonder why she backed off like that?"

"Damned if I know," said Raider, relieved.

"Something damned funny about it." He looked back through a crack in the door. "They maybe're gonna wait for some help. That posse, likely."

"So now what?"

"We get the hell out, that's what."

"We'll be spotted out in the open."

Stamper laughed harshly. He picked up his gear and walked to the back of the cave. Raider hadn't noticed the blanket hanging on the rear wall. Now Hobie swept it aside and stepped into a dark hole.

"Blow out that lamp," he said, "and foller me."

Raider picked up his gear and blew out the lamp. He

followed Hobie by the sound of the man's breathing, his grunts.

"What is this?" he asked.

"An excape tunnel," he said, mispronouncing the word "escape." "We'll be miles away afore they figger we're done gone."

Raider was impressed. They emerged on the other side of the ridge some moments later.

He saw another farmhouse, a barn, outbuildings. He followed Hobie dumbly as he walked toward the barn. He looked behind him. The entrance to the tunnel was almost invisible from all but a few feet away.

Before they reached the barn, Hobie made an odd call. He cupped his hands together and blew into them. The sound that he created was a perfect imitation of a dove's hollow moan. He worked one hand up and down to vary the pitch.

A figure stepped out of the barn leading three horses.

Hobie broke off the call and grinned.

"Howdy, Betty Sue," he said.

Betty Sue Summerfield smiled and walked up to them with three fresh horses.

"Someone after you?" she asked.

"I reckon," said Hobie. "Val Drews come up with them two sniffers and she had a city dude with her. Looked like the law."

Betty Sue frowned. Then she saw the look of surprise on Raider's face and laughed.

"You didn't think Seth left anything to chance, did you?" she chided.

"I reckon not," said Raider. "What about Molly and the horses on the other side?"

"Oh, Molly's long gone," she said. "She's got your route all set up for you."

"Where now?" Raider knew now why no one had managed to track Mantooth or his men. The countryside was one big maze to trackers, but the outlaws knew every nook and cranny.

"Seth wants to lay low after this one. Let the dust settle. He said if you boys came out this side to tell you to split up. Hobie, you know where to go. I'll take Jess here and point him in the right direction."

"Betty Sue," warned Hobie. "You know what Seth said."

"I know," she said impatiently. "I won't take him back to my place."

Hobie took the reins of one of the horses. In a few moments he was gone. Betty Sue handed the reins of another horse to Raider.

"Here, Jess. I can ride with you a ways. Seth's real strict. When he gives orders, we got to follow 'em."

"I understand."

They rode off together, heading east. Hobie had headed south, presumably to join up with Mantooth. Raider felt defeated. He was no closer to learning where Mantooth's main hideout was than before. He gathered that he'd be on his own once Betty Sue left him. And he figured that so far as Mantooth was concerned, he was completely expendable. It wouldn't make any difference to the outlaw whether he made it or not.

"No one knows you yet," Betty Sue told him after they'd put a couple of miles behind them. The sun was just hanging on the top of a distant ridge. In a moment it would disappear and the darkness would settle over the mysterious Ozark hills. "Seth says you're to come back to my place in a week and he'll meet up with you. It's big this time."

"Big?"

Betty Sue laughed.

"You'll find out," she said. "Seth, he's going to be a hero."

"How?"

"No, I can't tell you yet. Seth will. In a week."

"Where am I supposed to go for a week?"

Betty Sue pressed some bills in his hand.

"There's a little hiding place up on the road between Alpena and Harrison, if you find a posse on your trail. Little white house on the side of the road. Nobody lives there. It's got a hidey-cellar out back. Two box elders in front, some redbuds and dogwoods in the back. Some plum trees. You can't miss it. If I can, I'll come see you in five days."

"Why five days?"

"I've got to do some visiting," she said.

"Visiting?"

She laughed again and squeezed his hand.

"The 'Lend and Take,' silly."

"I don't know what that is."

"That's the enemy. Seth's enemy. Our enemy."

Before he could ask her more, she leaned over and kissed him. Then she clapped heels into her horse's flanks and rode off.

"'Bye," she said. "Just head north and you'll be in Capps. Stay away from Harrison for a week."

"Wait, Betty Sue. Damn it! Betty Sue."

But she didn't wait. She turned once and waved, then disappeared in a hollow draw that swallowed her up.

Raider wondered whether he should try to follow her. He decided against it. Hobie was already a little suspicious over what had happened back at the springhouse. Mantooth was no fool. It wouldn't take much to make him turn on his newest man. No, Raider would play it straight this time.

He had a week. Five days at least.

Time enough to go to Hollister and see if Doc had any messages for him. Or leave one for Doc. With Charlie.

One thing was sure—something big was up. Bigger than

either he or Doc could imagine. It was no simple robbery. There would be dynamite used, he was certain. And more bloodshed.

The robbery that morning showed Mantooth's determination. It broke the pattern. No longer was Mantooth a Robin Hood riding the countryside and through the forests, stealing from the rich to feed the poor. He was a man bent on some terrible vengeance against an enemy Raider did not know. Maybe Doc had learned something. Maybe he would know what "lend and take" meant.

Raider turned his horse into the gathering dusk. Soon he came to a road. When the stars came out, he followed the North Star.

Something ominous was in the wind.

His thoughts weighed heavy on his mind.

And Mantooth was still just beyond his grasp, bent on some terrible vengeance, armed with some horrible plan that Raider could not fathom.

But somewhere in the back of his mind, clawing for recognition, was the answer to some of his questions. He knew he must have missed something important somewhere. Something that would tell him what Mantooth planned to do.

The whippoorwills started up, calling through the woods.

Their speech made no sense to Raider either.

CHAPTER SEVENTEEN

Doc kept staring at the ridge across the way, watching the shadows pull along its length as the sun went down.

"Val," he said, "look at this, will you?"

The woman, with other things on her mind, turned and followed Doc's pointing finger with her eyes.

"I don't see anything unusual," she said.

"That ridge over there. Where the hideout is. See how it tapers down? It looks thin. I just wonder if that hole in the hill doesn't have a back door."

"It might," she said.

"Come on!" he exclaimed. "We're wasting time."

"Wait a minute."

But Doc was already running toward his borrowed horse, hoping he wasn't too late.

The dogs raced through the cave, reaching the other side as the sun went down over the far hills.

"You were right, Doc," said Val. "Better get the horses and ride around to the other side. I'll meet you there."

Doc wasted no time in backing out of the room where Raider and one of the outlaws had been a short time before.

He led Val's horse as he rode around the short end of the ridge. The faint light lingered on. He saw Val and her two dogs waiting for him by the barn.

"They were here," she said when he rode up.

"I could kick myself."

"Some of these slave hideouts were pretty slick," she said.

"Now what?"

"The dogs can track in the dark. I have food for them. Do you want to go on?"

"For a ways," he said.

Val turned the dogs loose again and mounted up. They rode to a place where the dogs started racing around in circles, seemingly confused. Val dismounted. It was now quite dark.

"They split up here," she said. "Three people, I figure."

"How do you know that?"

"The dogs. They've showed me three separate trails. One goes north, one east, and the other south."

Doc stepped out of the saddle. He gave Val Raider's shirt again.

"I don't want to follow the owner of this shirt," he said. "Just the one who was back at the robbery. Can your dogs tell us the difference?"

"I—I think so," she said.

She knelt, letting the dogs sniff the shirt. They moved out on the north path. She called them back, put their leashes on. She gave Doc back the shirt.

"The owner of the shirt went north," she said.

She led them past the place where they circled. The dogs didn't follow the trail east but set out south. She held up and called to Doc.

"That's the way. I don't know who the other person is, but the dogs don't seem interested. I'd say one of the robbers went thataway."

"That's good enough for me. But you better keep the dogs close. I don't want to run up on that man in the dark."

"What do you figure on doing?"

"Follow for another hour, then wait it out until daylight."

"The scent's pretty strong, I'd say." The dogs were straining to be off on the track again.

"Good. Maybe we won't lose him this time."

Mantooth listened patiently to Hobie Stamper's report. He said nothing until the man had finished talking.

"You say this Jess Skaggs acted funny when Val Drews called off her dogs?"

"Yeah. Like he was glad or something."

"Hell, I'd be glad too. That doesn't tell me a lot, Stamper."

"I was going to throw down on that slicker. I think maybe Skaggs knew him."

Mantooth chewed on his underlip. He toyed with a half-dozen fuses cut to different lengths. The tabletop in the Limestone cabin was littered with coils of fuses, dynamite caps, and rolls of heavy twine. The men sat around the table, smoking and chewing tobacco.

"Anything else?"

"I don't like them dogs. I had the feeling all the way down here that they was just behind me."

"You see anybody?"

"Nope. I looked, though. I felt like I was being follered."

"Shit," said Benteen. "You're always like that."

"Did anyone follow you?" asked Mantooth pointedly.

"No. I'd swear it. It was just a feeling."

"The man with the derby," said Seth. "We got a pretty good idea who he is. Pinkerton man. He's the one who talked to Dover, right Molly?"

Molly had just cleaned up the breakfast dishes and was sitting with her husband, Norville, sipping coffee.

"He's the one. He's a Pinkerton all right. When I think of how close I came to getting caught by him I just shudder."

"So," said Mantooth, "what do we do now? Maybe this Skaggs is who he says he is, and maybe he isn't. We can't take a chance. Not now. We've got to know for sure."

Molly spoke up then.

"Betty Sue could find out," she said. "She likes him, but she's loyal."

"Damned right," said Norville. "Betty Sue could find out real quick."

"Get the word to her," said Mantooth. "We've got less'n a week before we hit. Boys, we got some plans to lay out. Hobie, you set up another big meeting up at the junction store. Four days from now. Molly, you talk to Betty Sue. Tell her to play it natural. If this Skaggs is a detective, I want his ass."

Doc let out a cautious breath. From his position next to the cabin he could hear every word.

Val was well on her way back to Carrollton to get the Studebaker. In fact, she might even be there by now. They had caught sight of the man he now knew to be called Hobie, and Doc had realized that they were being led to Mantooth's hideout. Once he had realized that he would no longer need the dogs, he had sent Val and her two hounds back to Carrollton. Hobie had not been difficult to track. The man had ridden hard, making a beeline for the hideout. Doc could hardly believe his good luck. At the same time, he was conscious of the extreme danger he was in. in the middle of the outlaw camp, he was vulnerable. One mistake and he was a dead man.

Now, after listening to Mantooth, he knew that Raider's life expectancy had been considerably shortened.

And his as well.

Doc slunk backwards to the creek. He walked upstream, despite his aversion to getting his feet wet, dirtying his shoes and trousers. He was beyond that now. His face had two days of beard stubble sprouting from it; his clothes were unkempt and stank of sweat. He hadn't eaten since the previous sunset, when one of the dogs had captured a rabbit. Val had cooked it to a juicy turn over coals. They had made love in a cedar grove.

Now he was alone, and he had to put distance between himself and the outlaw camp.

He found a place where he could watch the road but not be seen. Soon after he was settled he saw Molly ride out. Like a nail in Raider's coffin, he thought.

Tonight, he vowed, he'd sneak back down to the main cabin under cover of darkness to see if he could learn any more. He had already seen the dynamite and knew Mantooth had something big planned. But what?

And where was the meeting to be held? A meeting with whom?

Doc sighed.

He knew so much now, and so little.

And the waiting was hell.

There was no word from Doc in Hollister.

But Charlie had a puzzling message for Raider.

"If you see Doc, give him these," said Charlie. "Came in this morning's post. I opened them and memorized them."

Jobs had already told Raider about the shoot-out and about Clemson snooping around. "I think Doc expected them. He told me to open his mail if he wasn't here."

Raider, worn out from the hard ride north, slumped in a chair at one of the Red Lion's tables. He opened the envelope, which was addressed to Weatherbee, Red Lion Tavern, Hollister, Missouri.

"Bring me the biggest, coolest beer you got, Charlie," said Raider.

"You got it."

Raider read the telegram. It was long, even for Wagner.

> AUTOPSY SPRINGFIELD REVEALS BODY NOT AS IDENTIFIED STOP DUANE BEALE OKAY STOP OTHER MAN IS NOT REPEAT NOT PAUL STONE STOP POSITIVE STONE STILL AT LARGE STOP VERY IMPORTANT YOU BRING IN MANTOOTH STOP DEAD MAN IDENTIFIED AS WAYNE MICHAEL BOOTH STOP BOOTH COURIER FOR OZARK LAND AND TRUST COMPANY STOP MAIN OFFICE SPRINGFIELD STOP HIGHLY TRUSTED STOP IMPERATIVE YOU BRING FAST ARRESTS THIS CASE STOP A P INSISTS SOONEST STOP WAGNER

Charlie Jobs brought the beer and sat down. The Red Lion was empty except for the two men.

"What do you make of it?" the undercover barman asked.

"Hell of a thing. You and Doc thought that was Stone?"

"Doc did. The man said he was Stone."

"What's this Ozark Land and Trust?"

"Bank. There's one here. They're all over."

"What do they do?"

"Loan money on land. To farmers, homesteaders."

Raider swallowed half a glassful of beer in one gulp.

"So," he said aloud, but to himself, "what's a bank courier doing in a shoot-out with you and Doc? And what's his connection with Beale? And Mantooth?"

"What's your drift, Raider?"

Raider finished the glass of beer and wiped his lips.

"Something just doesn't ring right. Beale looked at that bank pretty hard the day I came down with him. It didn't mean much at the time."

"Does it now?"

Raider thought back to that night at the meeting, when he had met Betty Sue and Mantooth. Mantooth hinted that something big was afoot. Now it appeared that a trusted employee of a bank was somehow involved with the outlaw band. What was the connection? Was there a connection?

"I don't know, Charlie. What do you know about that bank?"

"Not much. Main office is in Springfield. I've heard people in here talk about it after they've had a few."

Raider's eyes glittered with interest. He leaned forward, his features hardening to an intensity that startled Charlie.

"Tell me what you heard. Everything."

Charlie leaned back in his chair and searched his mind.

"Not much to tell. Bank sprung up after the war. It was part of Reconstruction, I guess. Loaned money to help folks get back on their feet. Spread down into Arkansas. Seems to be prospering."

"No, that's not what I want to hear. What do the people say about the bank? Do they like the way they do business?"

Charlie's eyes widened.

"Say, you're not too dumb, are you, Raider? I know what you mean. Sure, there's been a lot of talk. I put it down to grumbling, but..."

"But what? Damn it, Charlie..."

"Okay. From what I've heard, the Missourians like the bank. Some of the locals are stockholders. They even brag about it, when they're by themselves. But the Arkansaw-yers, they say different."

"What different?"

"Oh, they say the Ozark Lend and Take has just about cleaned them out of house and home."

Raider almost leaped across the table at Charlie.

"What did you just say?" he asked.

"I said the bank—"

"No, you said something else. What did you call it? The name of the bank?"

"Ozark Lan . . . oh, that. They call it the Lend and Take down in Arkansas."

"Christ," said Raider. "There it is."

"What?"

"Damn it, I've got to find Doc. If I miss him, you tell him I'll be at the Jasper crossroads, Clemson's store. Tell him to bring every gun he can."

Charlie stared at Raider in abject stupefaction.

"What's going on?"

Raider started for the door.

"I just found out what Mantooth plans to do. You better get word up to Springfield. Get in touch with the sheriff there, Wales is his name. Tell him something big's up and to start lining up good men who can shoot."

"Want me to tell him anything about the bank?"

"Not a word," said Raider.

"Where are you going?"

"To find a man named Paul Stone."

Betty Sue was waiting at the abandoned house on the Alpena-Harrison road. Raider rode up quietly and hitched his horse out back. He wouldn't be there long.

He went in without knocking.

Betty Sue rose up from the divan.

The minute he saw her he knew she had a pretty good idea who he really was. She smiled too broadly. Her eyes flickered, avoiding direct contact with his.

"Oh, Jess, I was worried about you," she cooed. "Where have you been?"

"Hollister?"

Her face went blank.

"Hollister? Whatever for? I've been waiting for you."

She was pretty. She had her hair tied back. Her dress was clean and fresh. She smelled of honey and wildflowers and cedar.

Raider strode up to her and grasped her wrists.

He squeezed. Hard.

"Jess Skaggs! Please! You're hurting me."

"I want some answers, Betty Sue. Quick. I might break your arms if you don't talk fast enough."

"Who—who are you?" she gasped.

"Never mind that. I want Paul Stone."

"Paul . . . I—I don't know what you're talking about."

Raider twisted her wrists and squeezed even harder.

Betty Sue cried out in pain.

"D-don't!" she pleaded.

"Paul Stone. Where is he?"

"I—I don't know! Honest. No one does. Seth, he sent Norville looking for him. Nobody knows what happened to him."

Raider knew she was lying. Oh, he believed that she was telling the truth about not knowing where Paul Stone was right now. But there was something else there, something he couldn't put his finger on, something just out of reach. He decided on another tack.

He relaxed the pressure on her wrists.

"Tell me about Paul Stone. What does he look like?

Where does he figure in all this? Is that his real name?"

Betty Sue's face drained suddenly of color. Her lips quivered. She opened her mouth, but no sound came out.

"Tell me," he said tightly, "or I'll snap your wrists like twigs."

The woman opened her mouth again, but again no sound came out.

Instead there was a thundering roar at the window. A pane shattered, spraying glass into the room.

Betty Sue sagged as her knees buckled.

Raider turned and tried to peer through the thick cloud of white smoke. He loosened his grip on Betty Sue's wrists and grabbed for her waist. His left hand felt something sticky, wet.

"Oooooh," she moaned.

The bullet had entered her body just under her right armpit, shattering ribs.

"Betty Sue," Raider croaked.

Her eyes misted and turned glassy. He let her down gently, feeling the blood pump onto his hand.

He drew his pistol, anger blazing in his eyes. His jaw tightened with rage.

A face appeared through the drifting layers of smoke. Raider cocked as he brought his pistol up. He had only a split second to fire. The man shouldn't have stayed there. It was too late for him. Raider was fast. Deadly fast.

He fired at the face and saw a dark depression form between the eyes before the smoke obscured his vision. Raider's ears filled with the boom of the explosion.

Hobie Stamper made no sound as he dropped, dead before his crumpling body struck the ground.

Betty Sue moaned in pain. Raider squatted beside her.

"Can you hear me?" he asked, a thick frog in his throat.

"Yes."

"You haven't got much time. Tell me where I can find Paul Stone. Tell me who he is."

Her eyes frosted over with the pale glaze of impending death.

"Paul Stone," she gasped, "lives...

Her throat rattled, and her eyes closed.

Raider felt the air in his lungs thicken. He touched a spot under Betty Sue's left ear, feeling for the pulse. It was like touching cold soft wax. There was no pulse, no heartbeat.

Betty Sue was dead, the secret of Paul Stone locked in her still heart.

CHAPTER EIGHTEEN

Doc waited two days for Val's return. During that time he lost ten pounds and gained much information.

He stayed awake until late at night and slept fitfully during the day. The two nights he listened at the cabin were by far the most valuable he had spent on the case.

He had ridden cautiously into Deer on two occasions to buy food, suffering the odd looks from townspeople reserved for outsiders and derelicts. Now, standing at the window, listening to Mantooth and his cronies eat supper, he was assailed with hunger pangs once again.

"Here's to Paul Stone," said Mantooth when the meal was over and the men were drinking brandy.

"Here, here!" said the others.

"Paul Stone lives!" exclaimed Norville Clemson.

Puzzled, Doc drew away from the window. He had witnessed the same ritual the night before.

And Paul Stone was dead, so far as he knew.

"Boys," said Mantooth, "in three days, the Lend and

Take will be brought to its knees. I figure we'll have the undying gratitude of the people."

"What then?" asked Lazarus Benteen.

"Why, we'll run things our way," replied Mantooth. "We'll have money, plenty of power."

Approaching hoofbeats warned Doc that someone was dropping in at that late hour. He shrank back in the shadows, glad that the outlaws felt so safe in their hideout that they didn't bother with guards. Otherwise he'd have been discovered long before.

The porch shook as someone walked to the front door and entered. No one seemed surprised. Doc hugged the wall, straining to hear. He wished he could see in, but that was a risk he was not prepared to take. Not yet.

"Quick trip," said Mantooth. "Hungry?"

"No," said a voice Doc recognized.

"How's Paul Stone?"

"Alive and well. Everything's set. The celebration's set for Friday. I have bad news, though."

Doc knew that Molly Clemson had been the one to ride up. The part about Paul Stone mystified him, however. She had said he was still breathing. Who then was the man he had killed in Hollister? And why did everyone defer to Stone, drink toasts to him, ask about his health?

"Set," said Mantooth. Doc heard a scraping chair. "You said something about bad news. Best go on and tell it."

Sounds of sobbing floated through the open window.

"It's Betty Sue. She ain't comin' back, Seth. She—she's dead. So's Hobie."

"How?" Mantooth's voice sounded like it issued from a tomb.

"Shot. Both of 'em. Luke Snodgrass come in with the report from the Lend and Take in Green Forest. He stopped at the safe house when he saw horses in the yard. He brought them in, Seth. Poor Betty Sue."

"Had to be that bastard Skaggs, you ask me," volunteered Benteen.

Doc had no idea who Skaggs was, but he had a pretty good idea that this was the name Raider had adopted. Skaggs had been discussed frequently the past few days.

There was more talk, then Seth asked Molly for a report. Doc listened attentively.

"Everybody's in place. You get the dynamite to them on Friday morning. I sent a message to Springfield, a false tip that you were going to hit a freight caravan coming down that morning. That ought to keep the law busy."

"The riders will go out Thursday night. We'll leave the same time."

"How many men will we have for the Springfield bank?" asked Norville.

"Thirty, at least," said Mantooth. "Ten at Hollister, the same at Forsyth. Ozark Land and Trust won't have any money-grubbing banks in Missouri when we get through with them."

"Or Arkansas either, for that matter," gloated Benteen. "We've got a hundred men ready to blow 'em to hell."

Doc had heard enough. He slipped away from the house. He could no longer wait for Val. He had to get to a telegraph immediately. The entire horror of Mantooth's plan began to take shape in his mind. Now he knew what "Lend and Take" meant. It was a slang term for the Ozark Land and Trust Company. There wasn't much time. If he was going to foil the outlaw's plans, he had to move fast.

Raider knew that if he waited long enough someone would discover the bodies. He recognized the man who strapped them to the horses as one he had seen at the junction the night he had met Mantooth. He followed him there and saw Molly leave that afternoon. He was right behind her.

Now, astride his horse, he saw a man in shadow run from behind the cabin. Raider drew his pistol and waited.

The man scrambled up the hillside, trying not to make noise.

Raider kicked the horse's flanks and cut the climber off.

"One move and you're dead," he whispered.

"Raider, is that you?"

"Doc?"

A sigh of relief.

The two men spoke briefly. Doc caught up his horse. Moments later they were riding up the steep grade out of Limestone.

"I've got to get the wagon from Val," Doc said as they rode along, "and get to the nearest telegraph pole."

"It's a good thing I followed Molly down here. I was certain she was making for the hideout."

"No time to get enough men together to stop Mantooth there. Besides, that place is a fortress. It would take a month to get them all out of there."

They rode west out of Deer, toward Swain.

"What do you figure on doing, Doc?"

"I don't know. We've got to warn Wales that he'll be getting a phony tip. He'll have to dispatch men to the banks up there. Tomorrow I'll see what we can do to alert the banks down here."

"It's a hell of a plan," admitted Raider.

"Mine or Mantooth's?"

"I was thinking of Mantooth's. It might could work."

Doc shuddered.

They caught up with Val and Rule Usrey just south of

Compton. The barking bloodhounds sounded the alarm. The wagon was pulled to the side of the road. Usrey challenged the two Pinkertons.

"Val, it's me, Doc."

A sleepy-eyed Val emerged from the wagon.

"We'll take it from here," Raider told Usrey.

Doc gave up his horse and made his apologies to Judith for abandoning her. Raider got a little sick at this display of affection. He hitched his horse to the back of the wagon.

"You go back to sleep, Val. How far is it to Harrison?"

"If we turn the wagon around, it's not far. Twenty-five miles or so. But some steep."

Usrey rode away, leading the horse he had loaned Doc.

"I reckon his evening was ruined," said Raider.

They didn't speak much on the drive to Harrison. It was slow going with Judith struggling up the hills and poking along on the way down. At dawn they reached the outskirts of Harrison. The treetops were just turning peach from the rays of the rising sun, the gray bluffs emerging out of shadow.

"Is there a telegraph office in Harrison?" asked Doc.

"It don't open till noon," said Val. "Some days."

Doc snapped the reins, rattling them atop Judith's back. The mule continued to plod at a steady pace, making less than five miles an hour.

"Raider, looks as though you'll have to do some climbing."

"I'm no monkey, Doc."

"We'll both be monkeys if you don't shinny up the first pole we spot." Doc turned his attention to Val, who sat in the back. "Val, want you to do me a favor. Deliver a message in Hollister. You can take Raider's horse."

"My horse?" protested Raider.

"Shut up, Raider."

* * *

After Val rode off on Raider's horse, the same one Doc had bought him in Springfield, her dogs happily leading the way, Raider turned to his partner with an accusing stare.

"You been plumbing that, Doc?"

"None of your business, Raider."

"I'd like to have seen that. Hope she kept the dogs chained up."

"Shut your mouth."

Raider laughed and stroked his beard. He would be glad to get out from behind it. There was no longer any need for a disguise. But he had gotten used to the horse. Not a good horse, but it grew on a man.

Doc found a telegraph pole northwest of town that wasn't too conspicuous. Luckily, there was not much traffic at that hour.

Raider stretched his legs as Doc climbed into the back of the Studebaker. He wondered why people didn't nail two-by-fours to the poles so someone could climb the damned things.

Doc rolled up the oriental rug covering the concealed hatch in the wagon bed. He pulled a countersunk handle and raised the secret door. His fingers groped for the hidden supplies. Grunting, he pulled out a standard Western Union solid steel lever and trunnion, nickel-plated, and a six-by-eight gravity battery. The battery weighed seven pounds and was constructed of zinc, copper, lead, and blue vitriol. He took out enough wire and some climbing spikes.

Moments later, Raider, the spikes strapped to his boots, was grimly climbing the pole, his teeth clamped on the connecting wires. He made the connection and waved down to Doc.

Doc connected the wires to the battery and cranked it

up. Then he set up his key and began transmitting at thirty words a minute.

TO SHERIFF EDWIN WALES SPRINGFIELD STOP UR-
GENT YOU WARN MANAGERS OF ALL OZARK LAND AND
TRUST BANKS STOP MANTOOTH SET TO ROB ALL
BRANCHES ON FRIDAY MORNING STOP CHECK WITH
PINKERTON NATIONAL DETECTIVE AGENCY STOP SIGNED
WEATHERBEE

Then Doc sent another message, routing it directly to Wagner in Chicago.

LOCATED MANTOOTH HQ STOP UNABLE TO APPRE-
HEND STOP NOTIFYING LOCAL LAW ENFORCEMENT PLAN
TO ROB OZARK LAND AND TRUST BANKS MISSOURI AR-
KANSAS STOP NEED INFORMATION ON PAUL STONE LAT-
EST STOP MORE THAN 100 OUTLAWS DUE TO STRIKE
FRIDAY MORNING STOP PLEASE ADVISE STOP WEATH-
ERBEE

Raider, impatient, looked down at the top of Doc's derby.
"What the hell you doing, Doc? Writing a damned book."
Doc stopped transmitting and pulled out a cheroot. He lit it and stared up at Raider.
"I'm still stumped about Paul Stone."
"I showed you the message I got from Charlie."
"There's still some doubt."
"Hell, Doc, maybe there isn't any Paul Stone. Maybe it's just—"
The cheroot almost fell from Doc's mouth.
"What were you going to say?"
"Maybe it's just a name Mantooth used. Or Beale. Maybe

there never was a Paul Stone."

"No, there was a Paul Stone. He was in the dossier. One of the original bunch."

"All right. Anybody you know ever see him? Did you ever see him?"

Doc tried to think back to when he questioned Dover. He couldn't remember the name Stone ever being mentioned. Someone, maybe it was Beale, or it could have been Sheriff Wales, had said that Stone spent a lot of time in Harrison.

"He's got an office here," Doc said suddenly. "Harrison Cartage Company. You can check that out while I talk to the local banker."

"Oh, no. I'll talk to the banker. You check the cartage company. I'm tired of the shit details."

Doc started to say something, but the key started clattering like gravel stones skidding down a washboard. He took out a pencil and pad and began writing furiously. Raider sighed. He didn't understand a single telegraph character.

MANTOOTH MUST BE STOPPED AND APPREHENDED SOONEST STOP NEW INFO ON PAUL STONE STOP

There was a pause. Doc waited impatiently, his pencil stub poised.

The key began chattering again.

PAUL STONE KILLED AT HELENA ARKANSAS JULY 4 1863 STOP BODY NOT CLAIMED STOP DISREGARD STONE STOP GET MANTOOTH AT ALL COSTS STOP WAGNER

Doc sent a quick reply.

ANY SURVIVORS PAUL STONE STOP WEATHERBEE

A few seconds later the di-da-dit began again.

STONE FAMILY BURNED OUT BY UNION FORCES STOP
LONE SURVIVOR SISTER STOP MOLLY WILSON STONE
AGE FIVE STOP WAGNER

Doc rattled the key, signing off.

"Jerk those wires. We hit pay dirt. There is no Paul Stone.
Not anymore. But Molly Clemson's his sister. She was a
kid when he was killed."

"Well, I'll be damned," said Raider, jerking loose the
wires.

"Mantooth's been using him as some kind of rallying
martyr."

A few moments later the two men were headed back to
Harrison. Doc laid out the plans.

"You'll have to get another horse and get to Springfield
as fast as you can. I'll warn the bankers here and join you
there."

"Can that mule make it in time?"

"Judith can walk faster than most horses, and she doesn't
get worn out like a horse that's pushed."

That made sense to Raider. Doc was seldom late for an
appointment.

"So we've been chasing a ghost," he said. "Paul Stone."

"Not really. I figure that Paul Stone meant something to
the men he fought with in the war. Mantooth and the others.
Maybe he was the reason they all turned outlaw in the first
place. Or perhaps he was the cause for those men to change
allegiance. After all, they rode with the Union in the beginning. Then they became Rebels. Maybe after the Stones

were burned out, killed in a fire."

"Makes sense. I guess it was pure hell down here," said Raider.

"It's going to be pure hell again if we don't stop it."

Raider nodded.

Mantooth, he decided, was not only a thief and a murderer, he was crazy.

And the crazy ones were the hardest to kill.

CHAPTER NINETEEN

Seth Mantooth looked at the tracks in the flickering light from the torch.

Norville Clemson swore softly.

Lazarus Benteen coughed.

"Looks like you were right, Norville," said Mantooth. "Somebody's been here listening to us."

"Couldn't have been gone long," said Benteen.

"Foller them tracks on out. I want to know if the spy is still here."

Clemson had sworn he'd heard hoofbeats up on the road. Mantooth had ordered a check, and now the proof was there by the window. Boot tracks. Seth walked back into the cabin while the two men, each carrying a torch, followed the tracks.

Molly was still awake, sitting at the kitchen table.

"Trouble?" she asked.

"Your old man was right. We've had ears for a day or two."

"Pinkertons?"

"Maybe. Can you get back tonight?"

"Seth, I'm worn out."

"We'll take the wagon in. You can sleep in the bed."

"With all that dynamite?"

"Just don't think about it. My hunch is it's that Weatherbee. If he's in Harrison, you can spot him for us."

"All right."

"We'll leave in an hour."

Doc was just finishing up the journal entry when the knock on the door came.

"Who is it?"

"Little Beau Peep."

Doc got up wearily from the table and walked to the door. He'd had three hours sleep, soaked in a tub for half an hour, and brushed the dust from his clothes.

"Come on in, Raider."

Raider, freshly shaved, had bathed and slept too. From the reek of his breath, Doc knew that he'd had an eye-opener as well.

"I'm ready to ride," said Raider. "Picked up a good horse from the livery."

"You had breakfast?"

"Such as it was. Cold grits, cold ham, runny eggs. You really pick the fine hotels, Doc."

"There wasn't much choice." Doc put away his journal and finished packing his valise. It was time to go. He drew his Waterbury from his watch pocket and read the face "Bank'll be open in half an hour."

"You don't have to wait around. They've probably got a telegram stuck in their door right now."

"Some loose ends, Raider."

"Hell, we've got this case licked."

Doc snapped the valise shut with a loud cracking sound.

"Not quite. Before you go, I want to give you something to think about. Have a chair."

Raider sat down at the table. He toyed with Doc's derby until the latter snatched it away.

"Shoot, Doc."

Weatherbee sat down and ran a finger around the curly brim of his derby.

"Something about this case has been bothering me all along," said Doc. "Ever since I first talked to Dover and Beale. Each turn in the road has presented more puzzles, deeper mysteries. And at every bend, another sign of a man that doesn't exist: Paul Stone. When I finished bringing my journal up to date a while ago it struck me that we've both missed something very important, a troubling aspect of this case that we should have addressed right from the beginning."

"I don't follow you, Doc. We followed every lead, checked out every clue. Allan Pinkerton himself couldn't have done better."

"Ah, that's not precisely correct. Throughout this case I've been impressed with several factors that have heightened my respect for Seth Mantooth, despicable as he may be."

"Doc, you're about to lose me with all those four-bit words. I've got a hell of a lot of riding to do and you want to ramble on like a schoolteacher. Get to the point."

"All right, Raider. Consider these two items: one, Mantooth knows about all important freight shipments out of Springfield; two, Mantooth has the ability to literally disappear when chased."

"So?"

"So this means he has a very vital communications network. And he has the support of a great many people.

Granted, he was a guerrilla during the war. Guerrilla warfare, to be effective, has to involve the people, noncombatants, a political consideration. Mantooth has preyed upon the people most affected by the outcome of the Civil War—the losers. He has orchestrated their feelings, their emotions, their desire for justice, for revenge. Will you grant me that?"

"That appears to be so, Doc. Again, what's the point?"

"Let's go back to communications for a moment. There was our first lead. And I missed it. Here was a freight outfit, presumably without blemish, that is suddenly hit. Even Beale played along. He hired an outside gun as a sacrificial lamb. I presume this was done to allay suspicions that Harrison Cartage and the Beale Security outfit were involved in previous robberies. But who is working at the freight outfit all of a sudden?"

"Molly Clemson."

"Molly Stone Clemson. Exactly!"

"That's bothered me too. A little."

"It should have bothered both of us a lot. As the French say, *Cherchez la femme*."

"Whatever that means, Doc," said Raider drily.

"It means that when a crime is committed, always look for a woman somewhere in the background. But Molly was right up there, square in front of our eyes. She was at Beale's when those men were blown up. She was at the meeting you attended. She brought messages and information to Mantooth at his hideout. She set up part of the escape route on the robbery in which you participated. In sum, she has been the thread that has linked every single move Mantooth has made. Molly has provided vital communications to this outlaw band and seems to know a great deal about the Ozark Land and Trust Company as well."

Raider let out a low whistle.

"By Billy damn, Doc, I think you might be right!"

"All we had to do was go after Molly and we'd have wrapped this up days ago."

"Well, it doesn't make much difference now."

"Doesn't it?"

"Go on, Doc. You're the dealer."

"I think Molly Clemson, using Paul Stone as a fictitious employer, or figurehead, is well embedded in the Ozark Land and Trust hierarchy. She may be a courier or an officer in the bank. But someone there has set things up, provided Mantooth with sufficient information to pull off this grandiose scheme of his."

Raider drew in a breath and narrowed his eyes. He could see it all now, just as Doc had laid it out. They should have gone after Molly from the beginning. Tear out Mantooth's communications network and he was like a blind man.

"What can we do about it now?" he asked Weatherbee.

"Not much. But if we want to wrap this case up right, then I'll have to dig into that bank and bring out some answers. That's where I'm going now. Harrison has been the center of Mantooth's operation. My guess is that Molly Clemson has an office and a desk at that bank. In fact, she may be sitting there right now, completing the final details of this mass robbery."

"Want some help?"

"No. See if Charlie has things set up. I'll see you in Springfield. I'm depending on you to coordinate the operations with the authorities."

Raider stood up and extended his hand.

"Doc, you bit off a chunk. I wish you luck. You'll need it. What's that French gobbledygook again?"

"Cherchez la femme."

"Yeah. Look out for the woman."

* * *

The Harrison branch of the Ozark Land and Trust Company bank was on the corner opposite the town square, on Vine and Rush. Doc hitched Judith across the street and walked over.

Inside, he strode to the enclosure. A male clerk looked up from his desk.

"The manager, please," said Weatherbee.

"May I ask what this is in regard to?"

"Police business."

"Yes, sir."

The clerk strode to a door and knocked. He disappeared inside. A few seconds later he reappeared.

"Right this way, sir." The clerk opened the gate, allowing Doc to enter. "Just go right in that door."

Doc walked in, prepared to state his case and find out what he could about Molly Clemson.

Two men rose from chairs and turned to face Doc. Beyond them, seated at the large desk, a figure in gray worsted stared out the window.

Doc swallowed hard.

Seth Mantooth and Norville Clemson reached out for him. Behind him, Lazarus Benteen closed the door quietly.

"You wanted to see the manager?" asked Mantooth with a leer.

The desk chair spun around.

Molly Clemson, neatly dressed in a tailored suit, looked at the Pinkerton.

"Good morning, Doc Weatherbee," she said. "I've been wondering when we'd meet."

Raider sweated in the morning sun. He glanced across the street for the hundredth time at the facade of the Ozark Land & Trust Company bank on Battlefield Road and Campbell. Sunlight dazzled the windows. People came and went. He looked around to see if any of the lawmen could be seen.

Everything was perfect.

Except where in hell was Weatherbee?

"Thought you said they was going to hit right after the bank opened?"

Raider turned around and looked at Sheriff Edwin Wales.

"Look, Wales, I showed you the telegram from Weatherbee. He said that was definite."

"Bank's been open for three hours."

"God damn it, I know that!"

Something was wrong. Raider had received the telegram last night. He had been relieved. Charlie Jobs, acting on instructions relayed by Val Drews, had met Raider in Hollister with a fresh mount. He had ridden like hell to Springfield and had organized constables, police, sheriffs, and marshals to guard all the banks due to be struck without showing themselves. Then the telegram, with Doc promising to be here before dawn.

Now, no Doc. No Mantooth.

Yes, something was damned sure wrong.

The day wore on. One of the deputies brought sandwiches. Raider listened to a lot of griping. His worries increased. A U.S. marshal came over and tapped the Pinkerton on the shoulder.

"It's been called off," he said.

"What's been called off?"

"The so-called robbery. We think you, the Pinkerton Agency, has led us all on a wild-goose chase."

"Bullshit."

"We're pulling our men."

Raider looked at the marshal in disgust.

"Wales? You pulling out too?"

"Bank's open another half hour or so. We'll stay."

Raider watched the marshal go. A few moments later, men who had been under cover began to walk away, carrying their rifles. More than a few of them looked over in Raider's direction, scowling.

"You put a lot of people to a lot of trouble, Raider," said Wales, rubbing his still-sore legs. "Next time, you better be sure of your facts."

"I am sure!"

"Yeah."

The minutes dragged by. Raider watched a shadow grow larger as the sun fell away in the sky. He was about to give it up himself. He shifted the Winchester rifle in his hands.

"Well, bank'll close in about ten minutes," said Wales. "No use tying up my men any longer."

"Okay, Wales. Thanks."

Wales started to leave and was about to give his men the high sign when he stopped.

"Say," he said. "Ain't that your man comin' up now? Weatherbee?"

Raider looked in the direction Wales was pointing.

Judith, pulling the Studebaker wagon, was plodding up Battlefield Road. Raider started to run out and greet Doc, when some instinct stopped him. The wagon drew closer.

"That's him," said Wales. "I recognize the derby, that fancy suit."

Raider stepped out in plain view. The man on the wagon lifted a hand. Judith kept coming.

"Doc?"

There was no reply. Raider wondered why Weatherbee didn't call out and engage in some friendly badinage.

"Hey, Doc, got a cigar?"

The man shrugged and shook his head.

Raider lifted the Winchester and cocked it.

"Hey! What the hell are you doing?" asked Wales.

The Pinkerton drew a bead on the man, hoping he was right. Once he had him in his sights, he was sure.

He held steady and squeezed the trigger.

The Winchester cracked like a whip. The man on the wagon rose up, a crimson stain on his shirt. He tumbled forward.

Then all hell broke loose.

A pack of men rode up on Campbell, wearing rough-out red boots, campaign hats, yellow dusters, screaming Rebel oaths. Gunfire erupted. Raider bent to one knee and began firing at the charging outlaws. Wales, too, began shooting. Puffs of smoke appeared from between buildings. People in the street scattered for cover.

Two men rode close to the bank carrying dynamite bundles. The fuses were lit. Raider dropped one. Bob Smith, from atop a building, dropped another. The fuses kept burning as the dynamite rolled into the middle of the road.

Mantooth charged straight for Raider.

The dynamite went off with a huge roar. Dust and debris rose up in a cloud.

Raider fired point-blank at the outlaw leader.

Mantooth screamed.

Lazarus Benteen charged for the bank.

Wales shot him out of the saddle.

Norville Clemson hurled a bundle of explosives at the bank window.

Raider rushed up and shot him in the face. He grabbed the bundle as it bounced off the wall and ripped out the fuse seconds before it reached the cap.

Men shouted. Rifles boomed.

It was over in a few minutes.

Doc was tied up in the back of the wagon. When Raider saw him in his silk underwear, he started laughing.

"Just wait, Raider. I'll get my turn."

Deputies began laying out the dead men, making identifications, bragging about the small war they had just waged.

Raider untied Doc, who immediately dug out a cheroot from a box in the back of the wagon.

"Where's Molly?" asked Raider.

"Right here," said a woman's voice.

Both men looked up and saw Molly astride a horse. She wore the same yellow duster, the campaign hat with the brim tied up on one side, the red rough-out boots. She held a rifle leveled at Doc's head.

There were tears in her eyes.

"Doc, you better say your prayers."

Raider knocked Doc down and swung his rifle up just as Molly fired. He squeezed the trigger. The hammer fell on an empty chamber. He threw the rifle at Molly, who swung her weapon for a shot at Raider. Raider drew his Remington .44 and thumbed it back. He fired. Molly gasped as the bullet struck her breast. She slid from the saddle. Doc got up and dusted himself off.

Raider grabbed the outlaw woman before she hit the ground. She was dying.

"We almost did it," she gasped.

"Almost," said Raider.

Her eyes glittered one last time.

Raider laid her out and shoved his pistol in its holster.

"You gonna put that in your journal, Doc?" he asked, disgustedly.

"It happened."

"I don't like killing a woman."

"That wasn't Molly you killed, you know."

"No? Who was it then?"

"Paul Stone. That's why she did all this. She kept him alive."

Raider drew a breath.

Well, now, he thought, maybe the man would stay dead.
He slapped Doc on the back.

There was no need to say anything.

Doc understood. Just as if he was a friend.

J.D. HARDIN

"THE MOST EXCITING WESTERN WRITER SINCE LOUIS L'AMOUR"
—JAKE LOGAN

____ 872-16840-9	BLOOD, SWEAT AND GOLD	$1.95
____ 872-16842-5	BLOODY SANDS	$1.95
____ 867-21039-7	SONS AND SINNERS	$1.95
____ 872-16869-7	THE SPIRIT AND THE FLESH	$1.95
____ 867-21226-8	BOBBIES, BAUBLES AND BLOOD	$2.25
____ 06572-3	DEATH LODE	$2.25
____ 06138-8	HELLFIRE HIDEAWAY	$2.25
____ 06380-1	THE FIREBRANDS	$2.25
____ 06410-7	DOWNRIVER TO HELL	$2.25
____ 06001-2	BIBLES, BULLETS AND BRIDES	$2.25
____ 06331-3	BLOODY TIME IN BLACKTOWER	$2.25
____ 06248-1	HANGMAN'S NOOSE	$2.25
____ 06337-2	THE MAN WITH NO FACE	$2.25
____ 06151-5	SASKATCHEWAN RISING	$2.25
____ 06412-3	BOUNTY HUNTER	$2.50
____ 06743-2	QUEENS OVER DEUCES	$2.50
____ 07017-4	LEAD LINED COFFINS	$2.50
____ 06845-5	SATAN'S BARGAIN	$2.50
____ 06850-1	THE WYOMING SPECIAL	$2.50
____ 07259-2	THE PECOS DOLLARS	$2.50
____ 07257-6	SAN JUAN SHOOTOUT	$2.50
____ 07379-3	OUTLAW TRAIL	$2.50
____ 07392-0	THE OZARK OUTLAWS	$2.50
____ 07461-7	TOMBSTONE IN DEADWOOD	$2.50
____ 07381-5	HOMESTEADER'S REVENGE	$2.50

Prices may be slightly higher in Canada.

B **BERKLEY**   *Available at your local bookstore or return this form to:*
Book Mailing Service
P.O. Box 690, Rockville Centre, NY 11571

Please send me the titles checked above. I enclose _____. Include 75¢ for postage and handling if one book is ordered; 25¢ per book for two or more not to exceed $1.75. California, Illinois, New York and Tennessee residents please add sales tax.

NAME _____

ADDRESS _____

CITY _____ STATE/ZIP _____

(allow six weeks for delivery.)